Tales From the Telling-House

R. D. Blackmore

Table of Contents

PREFACE.
　SLAIN BY THE DOONES.
　　CHAPTER I. AFTER A STORMY LIFE.
　　CHAPTER II. BY A QUIET RIVER.
　　CHAPTER III. WISE COUNSEL.
　　CHAPTER IV. A COTTAGE HOSPITAL.
　　CHAPTER V. MISTAKEN AIMS.
　　CHAPTER VI. OVER THE BRIDGE.
　FRIDA; OR, THE LOVER'S LEAP. A LEGEND OF THE
　WEST COUNTRY.
　　CHAPTER I.
　　CHAPTER II.
　　CHAPTER III.
　　CHAPTER IV.
　　CHAPTER V.
　　CHAPTER VI.
　　CHAPTER VII.
　　CHAPTER VIII.
　　CHAPTER IX.
　GEORGE BOWRING. A TALE OF CADER IDRIS.
　　CHAPTER I.
　　CHAPTER II.
　　CHAPTER III.
　　CHAPTER IV.
　　CHAPTER V.
　　CHAPTER VI.
　　CHAPTER VII.
　　CHAPTER VIII.
　CROCKER'S HOLE.
　　PART I.
　　PART II.
　　PART III.

PREFACE.

Sometimes of a night, when the spirit of a dream flits away for a waltz with the shadow of a pen, over dreary moors and dark waters, I behold an old man, with a keen profile, under a parson's shovel hat, riding a tall chestnut horse up the western slope of Exmoor, followed by his little grandson upon a shaggy and stuggy pony.

In the hazy folds of lower hills, some four or five miles behind them, may be seen the ancient Parsonage, where the lawn is a russet sponge of moss, and a stream tinkles under the dining-room floor, and the pious rook, poised on the pulpit of his nest, reads a hoarse sermon to the chimney-pots below. There is the home not of rooks alone, and parson, and dogs that are scouring the moor; but also of the patches of hurry we can see, and the bevies of bleating haste, converging by force of men and dogs towards the final *rendezvous*, the autumnal muster of the clans of wool.

For now the shrill piping of the northwest wind, and the browning of furze and heather, and a scollop of snow upon Oare-oak Hill, announce that the roving of soft green height, and the browsing of sunny hollow, must be changed for the durance of hurdled quads, and the monotonous munch of turnips. The joy of a scurry from the shadow of a cloud, the glory of a rally with a hundred heads in line, the pleasure of polishing a coign of rock, the bliss of beholding flat nose, brown eyes, and fringy forehead, approaching round a corner for a sheepish talk, these and every other jollity of freedom—what is now become of them? Gone! Like a midsummer dream, or the vision of a blue sky, pastured—to match the green hill—with white forms floating peacefully; a sky, where no dog can be, much less a man, only the fleeces of the gentle flock of heaven. Lackadaisy, and well-a-day! How many of you will be woolly ghosts like them, before you are two months older!

My grandfather knows what fine mutton is, though his

grandson indites of it by memory alone. "Ha, ha!" shouts the happier age, amid the bleating turmoil, the yelping of dogs, and the sprawling of shepherds; "John Fry, put your eye on that wether, the one with his J. B. upside down, we'll have a cut out of him on Sunday week, please God. Why, you stupid fellow, you don't even know a B yet! That is Farmer Passmore's mark you have got hold of. Two stomachs to a B; will you never understand? Just look at what you're doing! Here come James Bowden's and he has got a lot of ours! *Shep* is getting stupid, and deaf as a post. *Watch* is worth ten of him. Good dog, good dog! You won't let your master be cheated. How many of ours, John Fry? Quick now! You can tell, if you can't read; and I can read quicker than I can tell."

"Dree score, and vower Maister; 'cardin' to my rackonin'. Dree score and zax it waz as us toorned out, zeventh of June, God knows it waz. Wan us killed, long of harvest-taime; and wan tummled into bog-hole, across yanner to Mole's Chimmers."

"But," says the little chap on the shaggy pony, "John Fry, where are the four that ought to have R. D. B. on them? You promised me, on the blade of your knife, before I went to school again, that my two lambs should have their children marked the same as they were."

John turns redder than his own sheep's-redding. He knows that he has been caught out in a thumping lie, and although that happens to him almost every day, his conscience has a pure complexion still. "'Twaz along of the rains as wasshed 'un out." In vain has he scratched his head for a finer lie.

"Grandfather, you know that I had two lambs, and you let me put R. D. B. on them with both my hands, after the shearing-time last year, and I got six shillings for their wool the next time, and I gave it to a boy who thrashed a boy that bullied me. And Aunt Mary Anne wrote to tell me at school that my two lambs had increased two each, all of them sheep; and there was sure to be a lot of money soon for me. And so I went and promised it right and left, and how can I go back to school, and be called a liar? You call this the *Telling-house*, because people come here to tell their own sheep from their neighbours', when they fetch them home again. But I should say it was because they tell such stories here. And if that is the reason, I know who can tell the biggest ones."

With the pride of a conscious author, he blushes, that rogue of a John Fry blushes, wherever he has shaved within the last three weeks of his false life.

"Never mind, my boy; story-telling never answers in the end," says my Grandfather—oh how could he thus foresee my fate? "Be sure you always speak the truth."

That advice have I followed always. And if I lost my four sheep then, through the plagiarism of that bad fellow, by hook or crook I have fetched four more out of the wilderness of the past; and I only wish they were better mutton, for the pleasure of old friends who like a simple English joint.

R.D.B.
Old Christmas Day, 1896

SLAIN BY THE DOONES.
CHAPTER I.
AFTER A STORMY LIFE.

To hear people talking about North Devon, and the savage part called Exmoor, you might almost think that there never was any place in the world so beautiful, or any living men so wonderful. It is not my intention to make little of them, for they would be the last to permit it; neither do I feel ill will against them for the pangs they allowed me to suffer; for I dare say they could not help themselves, being so slow-blooded, and hard to stir even by their own egrimonies. But when I look back upon the things that happened, and were for a full generation of mankind accepted as the will of God, I say, that the people who endured them must have been born to be ruled by the devil. And in thinking thus I am not alone; for the very best judges of that day stopped short of that end of the world, because the law would not go any further. Nevertheless, every word is true of what I am going to tell, and the stoutest writer of history cannot make less of it by denial.

My father was Sylvester Ford of Quantock, in the county of Somerset, a gentleman of large estate as well as ancient lineage. Also of high courage and resolution not to be beaten, as he proved in his many rides with Prince Rupert, and woe that I should say it! in his most sad death. To this he was not looking forward much, though turned of threescore years and five; and his only child and loving daughter, Sylvia, which is myself, had never dreamed of losing him. For he was exceeding fond of me, little as I deserved it, except by loving him with all my heart and thinking nobody like him. And he without anything to go upon, except that he was my father, held, as I have often heard, as good an opinion of me.

Upon the triumph of that hard fanatic, the Brewer, who came to a timely end by the justice of high Heaven—my father, being disgusted with England as well as banished from her, and despoiled of all his property, took service on the Continent, and wandered there for many years, until the replacement of the throne. Thereupon he expected, as many others did, to get his estates restored to him, and perhaps to be held in high esteem at court, as he had a right to be. But this did not so come to pass. Excellent words were granted him, and promise of tenfold restitution; on the faith of which he returned to Paris, and married a young Italian lady of good birth and high qualities, but with nothing more to come to her. Then, to his great disappointment, he found himself left to live upon air—which, however distinguished, is not sufficient—and love, which, being fed so easily, expects all who lodge with it to live upon itself.

My father was full of strong loyalty; and the king (in his value of that sentiment) showed faith that it would support him. His majesty took both my father's hands, having learned that hearty style in France, and welcomed him with most gracious warmth, and promised him more than he could desire. But time went on, and the bright words faded, like a rose set bravely in a noble vase, without any nurture under it.

Another man had been long established in our hereditaments by the Commonwealth; and he would not quit them of his own accord, having a sense of obligation to himself. Nevertheless, he went so far as to offer my father a share of the land, if some honest lawyers, whom he quoted, could find proper means for arranging it. But my father said: "If I cannot have my rights, I will have my wrongs. No mixture of the two for me." And so, for the last few years of his life, being now very poor and a widower, he took refuge in an outlandish place, a house and small property in the heart of Exmoor, which had come to the Fords on the spindle side, and had been overlooked when their patrimony was confiscated by the Brewer. Of him I would speak with no contempt, because he was ever as good as his word.

In the course of time, we had grown used to live

according to our fortunes. And I verily believe that we were quite content, and repined but little at our lost importance. For my father was a very simple-minded man, who had seen so much of uproarious life, and the falsehood of friends, and small glitter of great folk, that he was glad to fall back upon his own good will. Moreover he had his books, and me; and as he always spoke out his thoughts, he seldom grudged to thank the Lord for having left both of these to him. I felt a little jealous of his books now and then, as a very poor scholar might be; but reason is the proper guide for women, and we are quick enough in discerning it, without having to borrow it from books.

At any rate now we were living in a wood, and trees were the only creatures near us, to the best of our belief and wish. Few might say in what part of the wood we lived, unless they saw the smoke ascending from our single chimney; so thick were the trees, and the land they stood on so full of sudden rise and fall. But a little river called the Lynn makes a crooked border to it, and being for its size as noisy a water as any in the world perhaps, can be heard all through the trees and leaves to the very top of the Warren Wood. In the summer all this was sweet and pleasant; but lonely and dreary and shuddersome, when the twigs bore drops instead of leaves, and the ground would not stand to the foot, and the play of light and shadow fell, like the lopping of a tree, into one great lump.

Now there was a young man about this time, and not so very distant from our place—as distances are counted there—who managed to make himself acquainted with us, although we lived so privately. To me it was a marvel, both why and how he did it; seeing what little we had to offer, and how much we desired to live alone. But Mrs. Pring told me to look in the glass, if I wanted to know the reason; and while I was blushing with anger at that, being only just turned eighteen years, and thinking of nobody but my father, she asked if I had never heard the famous rhymes made by the wise woman at Tarr-steps:

"Three fair maids live upon Exymoor, The rocks, and the woods, and the dairy-door. The son of a baron shall woo all three, But barren of them all shall the young man be."

Of the countless things I could never understand, one of the very strangest was how Deborah Pring, our only domestic, living in the lonely depths of this great wood, and seeming to see nobody but ourselves, in spite of all that contrived to know as much of the doings of the neighbourhood as if she went to market twice a week. But my father cared little for any such stuff; coming from a better part of the world, and having been mixed with mighty issues and making of great kingdoms, he never said what he thought of these little combings of petty pie crust, because it was not worth his while. And yet he seemed to take a kindly liking to the young De Wichehalse; not as a youth of birth only, but as one driven astray perhaps by harsh and austere influence. For his father, the baron, was a godly man,—which is much to the credit of anyone, growing rarer and rarer, as it does,—and there should be no rasp against such men, if they would only bear in mind that in their time they had been young, and were not quite so perfect then. But lo! I am writing as if I knew a great deal more than I could know until the harrow passed over me.

No one, however, need be surprised at the favour this young man obtained with all who came into his converse. Handsome, and beautiful as he was, so that bold maids longed to kiss him, it was the sadness in his eyes, and the gentle sense of doom therein, together with a laughing scorn of it, that made him come home to our nature, in a way that it feels but cannot talk of. And he seemed to be of the past somehow, although so young and bright and brave; of the time when greater things were done, and men would die for women. That he should woo three maids in vain, to me was a stupid old woman's tale.

"Sylvia," my father said to me, when I was not even thinking of him, "no more converse must we hold with that son of the Baron de Wichehalse. I have ordered Pring to keep the door; and Mistress Pring, who hath the stronger tongue, to come up if he attempted to dispute; the while I go away to catch our supper."

He was bearing a fishing rod made by himself, and a basket strapped over his shoulders.

"But why, father? Why should such a change be? How hath the young gentleman displeased thee?" I put my face into his beard as I spoke, that I might not appear too curious.

"Is it so?" he answered, "then high time is it. No more shall he enter this"—*house* he would have said, but being so truthful changed it into—"hut. I was pleased with the youth. He is gentle and kind; but weak—my dear child, remember that. Why are we in this hut, my dear? and thou, the heiress of the best land in the world, now picking up sticks in the wilderness? Because the man who should do us right is weak, and wavering, and careth but for pleasure. So is this young Marwood de Wichehalse. He rideth with the Doones. I knew it not, but now that I know, it is enough."

My father was of tall stature and fine presence, and his beard shone like a cascade of silver. It was not the manner of the young as yet to argue with their elders, and though I might have been a little fluttered by the comely gallant's lofty talk and gaze of daring melancholy, I said good-bye to him in my heart, as I kissed my noble father. Shall I ever cease to thank the Lord that I proved myself a good daughter then?

CHAPTER II.
BY A QUIET RIVER.

Living as we did all by ourselves, and five or six miles away from the Robbers' Valley, we had felt little fear of the Doones hitherto, because we had nothing for them to steal except a few books, the sight of which would only make them swear and ride away. But now that I was full-grown, and beginning to be accounted comely, my father was sometimes uneasy in his mind, as he told Deborah, and she told me; for the outlaws showed interest in such matters, even to the extent of carrying off young women who had won reputation thus. Therefore he left Thomas Pring at home, with the doors well-barred, and two duck guns loaded, and ordered me not to quit the house until he should return with a creel of trout for supper. Only our little boy Dick Hutchings was to go with him, to help when his fly caught in the bushes.

My father set off in the highest spirits, as anglers always seem to do, to balance the state in which they shall return; and I knew not, neither did anyone else, what a bold stroke he was resolved upon. When it was too late, we found out that, hearing so much of that strange race, he desired to know more about them, scorning the idea that men of birth could ever behave like savages, and forgetting that they had received no chance of being tamed, as rough spirits are by the lessons of the battlefield. No gentleman would ever dream of attacking an unarmed man, he thought; least of all one whose hair was white. And so he resolved to fish the brook which ran away from their stronghold, believing that he might see some of them, and hoping for a peaceful interview.

We waited and waited for his pleasant face, and long, deliberate step upon the steep, and cheerful shout for his Sylvia, to come and ease down his basket, and say—"Well done, father!" But the shadows of the trees grew darker, and the song of the gray-bird died out among them, and the silent wings of the owl swept by, and all the mysterious sounds of night in the depth of forest loneliness, and the glimmer of a star through the leaves here and there, to tell us that there still was light in heaven—but of an earthly father not a sign; only pain, and long sighs, and deep sinking of the heart.

But why should I dwell upon this? All women, being of a gentle and loving kind,—unless they forego their nature,—know better than I at this first trial knew, the misery often sent to us. I could not believe it, and went about in a dreary haze of wonder, getting into dark places, when all was dark, and expecting to be called out again and asked what had made such a fool of me. And so the long night went at last, and no comfort came in the morning. But I heard a great crying, sometime the next day, and ran back from the wood to learn what it meant, for there I had been searching up and down, not knowing whither I went or why. And lo, it was little Dick Hutchings at our door, and Deborah Pring held him by the coat-flap, and was beating him with one of my father's sticks.

"I tell 'ee, they Doo-uns has done for 'un," the boy was roaring betwixt his sobs; "dree on 'em, dree on 'em, and he've a killed one. The squire be layin' as dead as a sto-un."

Mrs. Pring smacked him on the mouth, for she saw that I had heard it. What followed I know not, for down I fell, and the sense of life went from me.

There was little chance of finding Thomas Pring, or any other man to help us, for neighbours were none, and Thomas was gone everywhere he could think of to look for them. Was I likely to wait for night again, and then talk for hours about it? I recovered my strength when the sun went low; and who was Deborah Pring, to stop me? She would have come, but I would not have it; and the strength of my grief took command of her.

Little Dick Hutchings whistled now, I remember that he whistled, as he went through the wood in front of me. Who had given him the breeches on his legs and the hat upon his shallow pate? And the poor little coward had skiddered away, and slept in a furze rick, till famine drove him home. But now he was set up again by gorging for an hour, and chattered as if he had done a great thing.

There must have been miles of rough walking through woods, and tangles, and craggy and black boggy hollows, until we arrived at a wide open space where two streams ran into one another.

"Thic be Oare watter," said the boy, "and t'other over yonner be Badgery. Squire be dead up there; plaise, Miss Sillie, 'ee can goo vorrard and vaind 'un."

He would go no further; but I crossed the brook, and followed the Badgery stream, without knowing, or caring to know, where I was. The banks, and the bushes, and the rushing water went by me until I came upon—but though the Lord hath made us to endure such things, he hath not compelled us to enlarge upon them.

In the course of the night kind people came, under the guidance of Thomas Pring, and they made a pair of wattles such as farmers use for sheep, and carried home father and daughter, one sobbing and groaning with a broken heart, and the other that should never so much as sigh again. Troubles have fallen upon me since, as the will of the Lord is always; but none that I ever felt like that, and for months everything was the same to me.

But inasmuch as it has been said by those who should know better, that my father in some way provoked his merciless end by those vile barbarians, I will put into plainest form, without any other change, except from outlandish words, the tale received from Dick Hutchings, the boy, who had seen and heard almost everything while crouching in the water and huddled up inside a bush.

"Squire had catched a tidy few, and he seemed well pleased with himself, and then we came to a sort of a hollow place where one brook floweth into the other. Here he was a-casting of his fly, most careful, for if there was ever a trout on the feed, it was like to be a big one, and lucky for me I was keeping round the corner when a kingfisher bird flew along like a string-bolt, and there were three great men coming round a fuzz-bush, and looking at squire, and he back to them. Down goes I, you may say sure enough, with all of me in the water but my face, and that stuck into a wutts-clump, and my teeth making holes in my naked knees, because of the way they were shaking.

"'Ho, fellow!' one of them called out to squire, as if he was no better than father is, 'who give thee leave to fish in our river?'

"'Open moor,' says squire, 'and belongeth to the king, if it belongeth to anybody. Any of you gentlemen hold his majesty's warrant to forbid an old officer of his?'

"That seemed to put them in a dreadful rage, for to talk of a warrant was unpleasant to them.

"'Good fellow, thou mayest spin spider's webs, or jib up and down like a gnat,' said one, 'but such tricks are not lawful upon land of ours. Therefore render up thy spoil.'

"Squire walked up from the pebbles at that, and he stood before the three of them, as tall as any of them. And he said, 'You be young men, but I am old. Nevertheless, I will not be robbed by three, or by thirty of you. If you be cowards enough, come on.'

"Two of them held off, and I heard them say, 'Let him alone, he is a brave old cock.' For you never seed anyone look more braver, and his heart was up with righteousness. But the other, who seemed to be the oldest of the three, shouted out something, and put his leg across, and made at the squire with a long blue thing that shone in the sun, like a looking-glass. And the squire, instead of turning round to run away as he should have, led at him with the thick end of the fishing rod, to which he had bound an old knife of Mother Pring's for to stick it in the grass, while he put his flies on. And I heard the old knife strike the man in his breast, and down he goes dead as a door-nail. And before I could look again almost, another man ran a long blade into squire, and there he was lying as straight as a lath, with the end of his white beard as red as a rose. At that I was so scared that I couldn't look no more, and the water came bubbling into my mouth, and I thought I was at home along of mother.

"By and by, I came back to myself with my face full of scratches in a bush, and the sun was going low, and the place all as quiet as Cheriton church. But the noise of the water told me where I was; and I got up, and ran for the life of me, till I came to the goyal. And then I got into a fuzz-rick, and slept all night, for I durstn't go home to tell Mother Pring. But I just took a look before I began to run, and the Doone that was killed was gone away, but the squire lay along with his arms stretched out, as quiet as a sheep before they hang him up to drain."

CHAPTER III.
WISE COUNSEL.

Some pious people seem not to care how many of their dearest hearts the Lord in heaven takes from them. How well I remember that in later life, I met a beautiful young widow, who had loved her husband with her one love, and was left with twin babies by him. I feared to speak, for I had known him well, and thought her the tenderest of the tender, and my eyes were full of tears for her. But she looked at me with some surprise, and said: "You loved my Bob, I know," for he was a cousin of my own, and as good a man as ever lived, "but, Sylvia, you must not commit the sin of grieving for him."

It may be so, in a better world, if people are allowed to die there; but as long as we are here, how can we help being as the Lord has made us? The sin, as it seems to me, would be to feel or fancy ourselves case-hardened against the will of our Maker, which so often is—that we should grieve. Without a thought how that might be, I did the natural thing, and cried about the death of my dear father until I was like to follow him. But a strange thing happened in a month or so of time, which according to Deborah saved my life, by compelling other thoughts to come. My father had been buried in a small churchyard, with nobody living near it, and the church itself was falling down, through scarcity of money on the moor. The Warren, as our wood was called, lay somewhere in the parish of Brendon, a straggling country, with a little village somewhere, and a blacksmith's shop and an ale house, but no church that anyone knew of, till you came to a place called Cheriton. And there was a little church all by itself, not easy to find, though it had four bells, which nobody dared to ring, for fear of his head and the burden above it. But a boy would go up the first Sunday of each month, and strike the liveliest of them with a poker from the smithy. And then a brave parson, who feared nothing but his duty, would make his way in, with a small flock at his heels, and read the Psalms of the day, and preach concerning the difficulty of doing better. And it was accounted to the credit of the Doones that they never came near him, for he had no money.

The Fords had been excellent Catholics always; but Thomas and Deborah Pring, who managed everything while I was overcome, said that the church, being now so old, must have belonged to us, and therefor might be considered holy. The parson also said that it would do, for he was not a man of hot persuasions. And so my dear father lay there, without a stone, or a word to tell who he was, and the grass began to grow.

Here I was sitting one afternoon in May, and the earth was beginning to look lively; when a shadow from the west fell over me, and a large, broad man stood behind it. If I had been at all like myself, a thing of that kind would have frightened me; but now the strings of my system seemed to have nothing like a jerk in them, for I cared not whither I went, nor how I looked, nor whether I went anywhere.

"Child! poor child!" It was a deep, soft voice of distant yet large benevolence. "Almost a woman, and a comely one, for those who think of such matters. Such a child I might have owned, if Heaven had been kind to me."

Low as I was of heart and spirit, I could not help looking up at him; for Mother Pring's voice, though her meaning was so good, sounded like a cackle in comparison to this. But when I looked up, such encouragement came from a great benign and steadfast gaze that I turned away my eyes, as I felt them overflow. But he said not a word, for his pity was too deep, and I thanked him in my heart for that.

"Pardon me if I am wrong," I said, with my eyes on the white flowers I had brought and arranged as my father would have liked them; "but perhaps you are the clergyman of this old church." For I had lain senseless and moaning on the ground when my father was carried away to be buried.

"How often am I taken for a clerk in holy orders! And in

better times I might have been of that sacred vocation, though so unworthy. But I am a member of the older church, and to me all this is heresy."

There was nothing of bigotry in our race, and we knew that we must put up with all changes for the worst; yet it pleased me not a little that so good a man should be also a sound Catholic.

"There are few of us left, and we are persecuted. Sad calumnies are spread about us," this venerable man proceeded, while I gazed on the silver locks that fell upon his well-worn velvet coat. "But of such things we take small heed, while we know that the Lord is with us. Haply even you, young maiden, have listened to slander about us."

I told him with some concern, although not caring much for such things now, that I never had any chance of listening to tales about anybody, and was yet without the honour of even knowing who he was.

"Few indeed care for that point now," he answered, with a toss of his glistening curls, and a lift of his broad white eyebrows. "Though there has been a time when the noblest of this earth—but vanity, vanity, the wise man saith. Yet some good I do in my quiet little way. There is a peaceful company among these hills, respected by all who conceive them aright. My child, perhaps you have heard of them?"

I replied sadly that I had not done so, but hoped that he would forgive me as one unacquainted with that neighbourhood. But I knew that there might be godly monks still in hiding, for the service of God in the wilderness.

"So far as the name goes, we are not monastics," he said, with a sparkle in his deep-set eyes; "we are but a family of ancient lineage, expelled from our home in these irreligious times. It is no longer in our power to do all the good we would, and therefore we are much undervalued. Perhaps you have heard of the Doones, my child?"

To me it was a wonder that he spoke of them thus, for his look was of beautiful mildness, instead of any just condemnation. But his aspect was as if he came from heaven; and I thought that he had a hard job before him, if he were sent to conduct the Doones thither.

"I am not severe; I think well of mankind," he went on, as I looked at him meekly; "perhaps because I am one of them. You are very young, my dear, and unable to form much opinion as yet. But let it be your rule of life ever to keep an open mind."

This advice impressed me much, though I could not see clearly what it meant. But the sun was going beyond Exmoor now, and safe as I felt with so good an old man, a long, lonely walk was before me. So I took up my basket and rose to depart, saying, "Good-bye, sir; I am much in your debt for your excellent advice and kindness."

He looked at me most benevolently, and whatever may be said of him hereafter, I shall always believe that he was a good man, overcome perhaps by circumstances, yet trying to make the best of them. He has now become a by-word as a hypocrite and a merciless self-seeker. But many young people, who met him as I did, without possibility of prejudice, hold a larger opinion of him. And surely young eyes are the brightest.

"I will protect thee, my dear," he said, looking capable in his great width and wisdom of protecting all the host of heaven. "I have protected a maiden even more beautiful than thou art. But now she hath unwisely fled from us. Our young men are thoughtless, but they are not violent, at least until they are sadly provoked. Your father was a brave man, and much to be esteemed. My brother, the mildest man that ever lived, hath ridden down hundreds of Roundheads with him. Therefore thou shalt come to no harm. But he should not have fallen upon our young men as if they were rabble of the Commonwealth."

Upon these words I looked at him I know not how, so great was the variance betwixt my ears and eyes. Then I tried to say something, but nothing would come, so entire was my amazement.

"Such are the things we have ever to contend with," he continued, as if to himself, with a smile of compassion at my prejudice. "Nay, I am not angry; I have seen so much of this. Right and wrong stand fast, and cannot be changed by any facundity. But time is short, and will soon be stirring. Have a backway from thy bedroom, child. I am Councillor Doone; by birthright and in right of understanding, the captain of that pious family, since the return of the good Sir Ensor to the land where there are no lies. So long as we are not molested in our peaceful valley, my will is law; and I have ordered that none shall go near thee. But a mob of country louts are drilling in a farmyard up the moorlands, to plunder and destroy us, if they can. We shall make short work of them. But after that, our youths may be provoked beyond control, and sally forth to make reprisal. They have their eyes on thee, I know, and thy father hath assaulted us. An ornament to our valley thou wouldst be; but I would reproach myself if the daughter of my brother's friend were discontented with our life. Therefore have I come to warn thee, for there are troublous times in front. Have a backway from thy bedroom, child, and slip out into the wood if a noise comes in the night."

Before I could thank him, he strode away, with a step of no small dignity, and as he raised his pointed hat, the western light showed nothing fairer or more venerable than the long wave of his silver locks.

CHAPTER IV.
A COTTAGE HOSPITAL.

Master Pring was not much of a man to talk. But for power of thought he was considered equal to any pair of other men, and superior of course to all womankind. Moreover, he had seen a good deal of fighting, not among outlaws, but fine soldiers well skilled in the proper style of it. So that it was impossible for him to think very highly of the Doones. Gentlemen they might be, he said, and therefore by nature well qualified to fight. But where could they have learned any discipline, any tactics, any knowledge of formation, or even any skill of sword or firearms? "Tush, there was his own son, Bob, now serving under Captain Purvis, as fine a young trooper as ever drew sword, and perhaps on his way at this very moment, under orders from the Lord Lieutenant, to rid the country of that pestilent race. Ah, ha! We soon shall see!"

And in truth we did see him, even sooner than his own dear mother had expected, and long before his father wanted him, though he loved him so much in his absence. For I heard a deep voice in the kitchen one night (before I was prepared for such things, by making a backway out of my bedroom), and thinking it best to know the worst, went out to ask what was doing there.

A young man was sitting upon the table, accounting too little of our house, yet showing no great readiness to boast, only to let us know who he was. He had a fine head of curly hair, and spoke with a firm conviction that there was much inside it. "Father, you have possessed small opportunity of seeing how we do things now. Mother is not to be blamed for thinking that we are in front of what used to be. What do we care how the country lies? We have heared all this stuff up at Oare. If there are bogs, we shall timber them. If there are rocks, we shall blow them up. If there are caves, we shall fire down them. The moment we get our guns into position— —"

"Hush, Bob, hush! Here is your master's daughter. Not the interlopers you put up with; but your real master, on whose property you were born. Is that the position for your guns?"

Being thus rebuked by his father, who was a very faithful-minded man, Robert Pring shuffled his long boots down, and made me a low salutation. But, having paid little attention to the things other people were full of, I left the young man to convince his parents, and he soon was successful with his mother.

Two, or it may have been three days after this, a great noise arose in the morning. I was dusting my father's books, which lay open just as he had left them. There was "Barker's Delight" and "Isaac Walton," and the "Secrets of Angling by J. D." and some notes of his own about making of flies; also fish hooks made of Spanish steel, and long hairs pulled from the tail of a gray horse, with spindles and bits of quill for plaiting them. So proud and so pleased had he been with these trifles, after the clamour and clash of life, that tears came into my eyes once more, as I thought of his tranquil and amiable ways.

"'Tis a wrong thing altogether to my mind," cried Deborah Pring, running in to me. "They Doones was established afore we come, and why not let them bide upon their own land? They treated poor master amiss, beyond denial; and never will I forgive them for it. All the same, he was catching what belonged to them; meaning for the best no doubt, because he was so righteous. And having such courage he killed one, or perhaps two; though I never could have thought so much of that old knife. But ever since that, they have been good, Miss Sillie, never even coming anigh us; and I don't believe half of the tales about them."

All this was new to me; for if anybody had cried shame and death upon that wicked horde, it was Deborah Pring, who was talking to me thus! I looked at her with wonder, suspecting for the moment that the venerable Councillor—who was clever enough to make a cow forget her calf—might have paid her a visit while I was away. But very soon the reason of the change appeared.

"Who hath taken command of the attack?" she asked, as if no one would believe the answer; "not Captain Purvis, as ought to have been, nor even Captain Dallas of Devon, but Spy Stickles by royal warrant, the man that hath been up to Oare so long! And my son Robert, who hath come down to help to train them, and understandeth cannon guns— —"

"Captain Purvis? I seem to know that name very well. I have often heard it from my father. And your son under him! Why, Deborah, what are you hiding from me?"

Now good Mrs. Pring was beginning to forget, or rather had never borne properly in mind, that I was the head of the household now, and entitled to know everything, and to be asked about it. But people who desire to have this done should insist upon it at the outset, which I had not been in proper state to do. So that she made quite a grievance of it, when I would not be treated as a helpless child. However, I soon put a stop to that, and discovered to my surprise much more than could be imagined.

And before I could say even half of what I thought, a great noise arose in the hollow of the hills, and came along the valleys, like the blowing of a wind that had picked up the roaring of mankind upon its way. Perhaps greater noise had never arisen upon the moor; and the cattle, and the quiet sheep, and even the wild deer came bounding from unsheltered places into any offering of branches, or of other heling from the turbulence of men. And then a gray fog rolled down the valley, and Deborah said it was cannon-smoke, following the river course; but to me it seemed only the usual thickness of the air, when the clouds hang low. Thomas Pring was gone, as behooved an ancient warrior, to see how his successors did things, and the boy Dick Hutchings had begged leave to sit in a tree and watch the smoke. Deborah and I were left alone, and a long and anxious day we had.

At last the wood-pigeons had stopped their cooing,—which they kept up for hours, when the weather matched the light,—and there was not a tree that could tell its own shadow, and we were contented with the gentle sounds that come through a forest when it falls asleep, and Deborah Pring, who had taken a motherly tendency toward me now, as if to make up for my father, was sitting in the porch with my hands in her lap, and telling me how to behave henceforth, as if the whole world depended upon that, when we heard a swishing sound, as of branches thrust aside, and then a low moan that went straight to my heart, as I thought of my father when he took the blow of death.

"My son, my Bob, my eldest boy!" cried Mistress Pring, jumping up and falling into my arms, like a pillow full of wire, for she insisted upon her figure still. But before I could do anything to help her— —

"Hit her on the back, ma'am; hit her hard upon the back. That is what always brings mother round," was shouted, as I might say, into my ear by the young man whom she was lamenting.

"Shut thy trap, Braggadose. To whom art thou speaking? Pretty much thou hast learned of war to come and give lessons to thy father! Mistress Sylvia, it is for thee to speak. Nothing would satisfy this young springal but to bring his beaten captain here, for the sake of mother's management. I told un that you would never take him in, for his father have taken in you pretty well! Captain Purvis of the Somerset I know not what—for the regiments now be all upside down. *Raggiments* is the proper name for them. Very like he be dead by this time, and better die out of doors than in. Take un away, Bob. No hospital here!"

"Thomas Pring, who are you," I said, for the sound of another low groan came through me, "to give orders to your master's daughter? If you bring not the poor wounded gentleman in, you shall never come through this door yourself."

"Ha, old hunks, I told thee so!"

The young man who spoke raised his hat to me, and I saw that it had a scarlet plume, such as Marwood de Wichehalse gloried in. "In with thee, and stretch him that he may die straight. I am off to Southmolton for Cutcliffe Lane, who can make a furze-fagot bloom again. My filly can give a land-yard in a mile to Tom Faggus and his Winnie. But mind one thing, all of you; it was none of us that shot the captain, but his own good men. Farewell, Mistress Sylvia!" With these words he made me a very low bow, and set off for his horse at the corner of the wood —as reckless a gallant as ever broke hearts, and those of his own kin foremost; yet himself so kind and loving.

CHAPTER V.
MISTAKEN AIMS.

Captain Purvis, now brought to the Warren in this very sad condition, had not been shot by his own men, as the dashing Marwood de Wichehalse said; neither was it quite true to say that he had been shot by anyone. What happened to him was simply this: While behaving with the utmost gallantry and encouraging the militia of Somerset, whose uniforms were faced with yellow, he received in his chest a terrific blow from the bottom of a bottle. This had been discharged from a culverin on the opposite side of the valley by the brave but impetuous sons of Devon, who wore the red facings, and had taken umbrage at a pure mistake on the part of their excellent friends and neighbours, the loyal band of Somerset. Either brigade had three culverins; and never having seen such things before, as was natural with good farmers' sons, they felt it a compliment to themselves to be intrusted with such danger, and resolved to make the most of it. However, when they tried to make them go, with the help of a good many horses, upon places that had no roads for war, and even no sort of road at all, the difficulty was beyond them. But a very clever blacksmith near Malmesford, who had better, as it proved, have stuck to the plough, persuaded them that he knew all about it, and would bring their guns to bear, if they let him have his way. So they took the long tubes from their carriages, and lashed rollers of barked oak under them, and with very stout ropes, and great power of swearing, dragged them into the proper place to overwhelm the Doones.

Here they mounted their guns upon cider barrels, with allowance of roll for recoil, and charged them to the very best of their knowledge, and pointed them as nearly as they could guess at the dwellings of the outlaws in the glen; three cannons on the north were of Somerset, and the three on the south were of Devonshire; but these latter had no balls of metal, only anything round they could pick up. Colonel Stickles was in command, by virtue of his royal warrant, and his plan was to make his chief assault in company with some chosen men, including his host, young farmer Ridd, at the head of the valley where the chief entrance was, while the trainbands pounded away on either side. And perhaps this would have succeeded well, except for a little mistake in firing, for which the enemy alone could be blamed with justice. For while Captain Purvis was behind the line rallying a few men who showed fear, and not expecting any combat yet, because Devonshire was not ready, an elderly gentleman of great authority appeared among the bombardiers. On his breast he wore a badge of office, and in his hat a noble plume of the sea eagle, and he handed his horse to a man in red clothes.

"Just in time," he shouted; "and the Lord be thanked for that! By order of His Majesty, I take supreme command. Ha, and high time, too, for it! You idiots, where are you pointing your guns? What allowance have you made for windage? Why, at that elevation, you'll shoot yourselves. Up with your muzzles, you yellow jackanapes! Down on your bellies! Hand me the linstock! By the Lord, you don't even know how to touch them off!"

The soldiers were abashed at his rebukes, and glad to lie down on their breasts for fear of the powder on their yellow facings. And thus they were shaken by three great roars, and wrapped in a cloud of streaky smoke. When this had cleared off, and they stood up, lo! the houses of the Doones were the same as before, but a great shriek arose on the opposite bank, and two good horses lay on the ground; and the red men were stamping about, and some crossing their arms, and some running for their lives, and the bravest of them stooping over one another. Then as Captain Purvis rushed up in great wrath, shouting: "What the devil do you mean by this?" another great roar arose from across the valley, and he was lying flat, and two other fine fellows were rolling in a furze bush without knowledge of it. But of the general and his horse there was no longer any token.

This was the matter that lay so heavily on the breast of Captain Purvis, sadly crushed as it was already by the spiteful stroke bitterly intended for him. His own men had meant no harm whatever, unless to the proper enemy; although they appear to have been deluded by a subtle device of the Councillor, for which on the other hand none may blame him. But those redfaced men, without any inquiry, turned the muzzles of their guns upon Somerset, and the injustice rankled for a generation between two equally honest counties. Happily they did not fight it out through scarcity of ammunition, as well as their mutual desire to go home and attend to their harvest business.

But Anthony Purvis, now our guest and patient, became very difficult to manage; not only because of his three broken ribs, but the lowness of the heart inside them. Dr. Cutcliffe Lane, a most cheerful man from that cheerful town Southmolton, was able (with the help of Providence) to make the bones grow again without much anger into their own embraces. It is useless, however, for the body to pretend that it is doing wonders on its own account, and rejoicing and holiday making, when the thing that sits inside it and holds the whip, keeps down upon the slouch and is out of sorts. And truly this was the case just now with the soul of Captain Purvis. Deborah Pring did her very best, and was in and out of his room every minute, and very often seemed to me to run him down when he deserved it not; on purpose that I might be started to run him up. But nothing of that sort told at all according to her intention. I kept myself very much to myself; feeling that my nature was too kind, and asking at some little questions of behaviour, what sort of returns my dear father had obtained for supposing other people as good as himself.

Moreover, it seemed an impossible thing that such a brave warrior, and a rich man too—for his father, Sir Geoffrey, was in full possession now of all the great property that belonged by right to us—that an officer who should have been in command of this fine expedition, if he had his dues, could be either the worse or the better of his wound, according to his glimpses of a simple maid like me. It was useless for Deborah Pring, or even Dr. Cutcliffe Lane himself, to go on as they did about love at first sight, and the rising of the heart when the ribs were broken, and a quantity of other stuff too foolish to repeat. "I am neither a plaster nor a poultice," I replied to myself, for I would not be too cross to them—and beyond a little peep at him, every afternoon, I kept out of the sight of Captain Purvis.

But these things made it very hard for me to be quite sure how to conduct myself, without father and mother to help me, and with Mistress Pring, who had always been such a landmark, becoming no more than a vane for the wind to blow upon as it listed; or, perhaps, as she listed to go with it. And remembering how she used to speak of the people who had ousted us, I told her that I could not make it out. Things were in this condition, and Captain Purvis, as it seemed to me, quite fit to go and make war again upon some of His Majesty's subjects, when a thing, altogether out of reason, or even of civilisation, happened; and people who live in lawful parts will accuse me of caring too little for the truth. But even before that came about, something less unreasonable—but still unexpected—befell me. To wit, I received through Mistress Pring an offer of marriage, immediate and pressing, from Captain Anthony Purvis! He must have been sadly confused by that blow on his heart to think mine so tender, or that this was the way to deal with it, though later explanations proved that Deborah, if she had been just, would have taken the whole reproach upon herself. The captain could scarcely have seen me, I believe more than half a dozen times to speak of; and generally he had shut his eyes, gentle as they were and beautiful; not only to make me feel less afraid, but to fill me with pity for his weakness. Having no knowledge of mankind as yet, I was touched to the brink of tears at first; until when the tray came out of his room soon after one of these pitiful moments, it was plain to the youngest comprehension that the sick man had left very little upon a shoulder of Exmoor mutton, and nothing in a bowl of thick onion sauce.

For that I would be the last to blame him, and being his hostess, I was glad to find it so. But Deborah played a most double-minded part; leading him to believe that now she was father and mother in one to me; while to me she went on, as if I was most headstrong, and certain to go against anything she said, though for her part she never said anything. Nevertheless he made a great mistake, as men always do, about our ways; and having some sense of what is right, I said, "Let me hear no more of Captain Purvis."

This forced him to leave us; which he might have done, for aught I could see to the contrary, a full week before he departed. He behaved very well when he said good-bye,—for I could not deny him that occasion,—and, perhaps, if he had not assured me so much of his everlasting gratitude, I should have felt surer of deserving it. Perhaps I was a little disappointed also, that he expressed no anxiety at leaving our cottage so much at the mercy of turbulent and triumphant outlaws. But it was not for me to speak of that; and when I knew the reason of his silence, it redounded tenfold to his credit. Nothing, however, vexed me so much as what Deborah Pring said afterward: that he could not help feeling in the sadness of his heart that I had behaved in that manner to him just because his father was in possession of our rightful home and property. I was not so small as that; and if he truly did suppose it, there must have been some fault on my part, for his nature was good to everybody, and perhaps all the better for not descending through too many high generations.

There is nothing more strange than the way things work in the mind of a woman, when left alone, to doubt about her own behaviour. With men it can scarcely be so cruel; because they can always convince themselves that they did their best; and if it fail, they can throw the fault upon Providence, or bad luck, or something outside their own power. But we seem always to be denied this happy style of thinking, and cannot put aside what comes into our hearts more quickly, and has less stir of outward things, to lead it away and to brighten it. So that I fell into sad, low spirits; and the glory of the year began to wane, and the forest grew more and more lonesome.

CHAPTER VI.
OVER THE BRIDGE.

The sound of the woods was with me now, both night and day, to dwell upon. Exmoor in general is bare of trees, though it hath the name of forest; but in the shelter, where the wind flies over, are many thick places full of shade. For here the trees and bushes thrive, so copious with rich moisture that, from the hills on the opposite side, no eye may pick holes in the umbrage; neither may a foot that gets amid them be sure of getting out again. And now was the fullest and heaviest time, for the summer had been a wet one, after a winter that went to our bones; and the leaves were at their darkest tone without any sense of autumn. As one stood beneath and wondered at their countless multitude, a quick breathing passed among them, not enough to make them move, but seeming rather as if they wished, and yet were half ashamed to sigh. And this was very sad for one whose spring comes only once for all.

One night toward the end of August I was lying awake thinking of the happier times, and wondering what the end would be—for now we had very little money left, and I would rather starve than die in debt—when I heard our cottage door smashed in and the sound of horrible voices. The roar of a gun rang up the stairs, and the crash of someone falling and the smoke came through my bedroom door, and then wailing mixed with curses. "Out of the way, old hag!" I heard, and then another shriek; and then I stood upon the stairs and looked down at them. The moon was shining through the shattered door, and the bodies and legs of men went to and fro, like branches in a tempest. Nobody seemed to notice me, although I had cast over my night-dress—having no more sense in the terror—a long silver coat of some animal shot by my father in his wanderings, and the light upon the stairs glistened round it. Having no time to think, I was turning to flee and jump out of my bedroom window, for which I had made some arrangements, according to the wisdom of the Councillor, when the flash of some light or the strain of my eyes showed me the body of Thomas Pring, our faithful old retainer, lying at the foot of the broken door, and beside it his good wife, creeping up to give him the last embrace of death. And lately she had been cross to him. At the sight of this my terror fled, and I cared not what became of me. Buckling the white skin round my waist, I went down the stairs as steadily as if it were breakfast time, and said:

"Brutes, murderers, cowards! you have slain my father; now slay me!"

Every one of those wicked men stood up and fixed his eyes on me; and if it had been a time to laugh, their amazement might have been laughed at. Some of them took me for a spirit— as I was told long afterward—and rightly enough their evil hearts were struck with dread of judgment. But even so, to scare them long in their contemptuous, godless vein was beyond the power of Heaven itself; and when one of my long tresses fell, to my great vexation, down my breast, a shocking sneer arose, and words unfit for a maiden's ear ensued.

"None of that! This is no farmhouse wench, but a lady of birth and breeding. She shall be our queen, instead of the one that hath been filched away. Sylvia, thou shalt come with me."

The man who spoke with this mighty voice was a terror to the others, for they fell away before him, and he was the biggest monster there—Carver Doone, whose name for many a generation shall be used to frighten unruly babes to bed. And now, as he strode up to me and bowed,—to show some breeding, —I doubt if the moon, in all her rounds of earth and sky and the realms below, fell ever upon another face so cold, repulsive, ruthless.

To belong to him, to feel his lips, to touch him with anything but a dagger! Suddenly I saw my father's sword hanging under a beam in the scabbard. With a quick spring I seized it, and, leaping up the stairs, had the long blade gleaming in the moonlight. The staircase would not hold two people abreast, and the stairs were as steep as narrow. I brought the point down it, with the hilt against my breast, and there was no room for another blade to swing and strike it up.

"Let her alone!" said Carver Doone, with a smile upon his cold and corpselike face. "My sons, let the lady have her time. She is worthy to be the mother of many a fine Doone."

The young men began to lounge about in a manner most provoking, as if I had passed from their minds altogether; and some of them went to the kitchen for victuals, and grumbled at our fare by the light of a lantern which they had found upon a shelf. But I stood at my post, with my heart beating, so that the long sword quivered like a candle. Of my life they might rob me, but of my honour, never!

"Beautiful maiden! Who hath ever seen the like? Why, even Lorna hath not such eyes."

Carver Doone came to the foot of the stairs and flashed the lantern at me, and, thinking that he meant to make a rush for it, I thrust my weapon forward; but at the same moment a great pair of arms was thrown around me from behind by some villain who must have scaled my chamber window, and backward I fell, with no sense or power left.

When my scattered wits came back I felt that I was being shaken grievously, and the moon was dancing in my eyes through mist of tears, half blinding them. I remember how hard I tried to get my fingers up to wipe my eyes, so as to obtain some knowledge; but jerk and bump and helpless wonder were all that I could get or take; for my hands were strapped, and my feet likewise, and I seemed like a wave going up and down, without any judgment, upon the open sea.

But presently I smelled the wholesome smell which a horse of all animals alone possesses, though sometimes a cow is almost as good, and then I felt a mane coming into my hair, and then there was the sound of steady feet moving just under me, with rise and fall and swing alternate, and a sense of going forward. I was on the back of a great, strong horse, and he was obeying the commands of man. Gradually I began to think, and understood my awful plight. The Doones were taking me to Doone Glen to be some cut-throat's light-of-love; perhaps to be passed from brute to brute—me, Sylvia Ford, my father's darling, a proud and dainty and stately maiden, of as good birth as any in this English realm. My heart broke down as I thought of that, and all discretion vanished. Though my hands were tied my throat was free, and I sent forth such a scream of woe that the many-winding vale of Lynn, with all its wild waters could not drown, nor with all its dumb foliage smother it; and the long wail rang from crag to crag, as the wrongs of men echo unto the ears of God.

"Valiant damsel, what a voice thou hast! Again, and again let it strike the skies. With them we are at peace, being persecuted here, according to the doom of all good men. And yet I am loth to have that fair throat strained."

It was Carver Doone who led my horse; and his horrible visage glared into my eyes through the strange, wan light that flows between the departure of the sinking moon and the flutter of the morning when it cannot see its way. I strove to look at him; but my scared eyes fell, and he bound his rank glove across my poor lips. "Let it be so," I thought; "I can do no more."

Then, when my heart was quite gone in despair, and all trouble shrank into a trifle, I heard a loud shout, and the trample of feet, and the rattle of arms, and the clash of horses. Contriving to twist myself a little, I saw that the band of the Doones were mounting a saddle-backed bridge in a deep wooded glen, with a roaring water under them. On the crown of the bridge a vast man stood, such as I had never descried before, bearing no armour that I could see, but wearing a farmer's hat, and raising a staff like the stem of a young oak tree. He was striking at no one, but playing with his staff, as if it were a willow in the morning breeze.

"Down with him! Ride him down! Send a bullet through him!" several of the Doones called out, but no one showed any hurry to do it. It seemed as if they knew him, and feared his mighty strength, and their guns were now slung behind their backs on account of the roughness of the way.

"Charlie, you are not afraid of him," I heard that crafty Carver say to the tallest of his villains, and a very handsome young man he was; "if the girl were not on my horse, I would do it. Ride over him, and you shall have my prize, when I am tired of her."

I felt the fire come into my eyes, to be spoken of so by a brute; and then I saw Charlie Doone spur up the bridge, leaning forward and swinging a long blade round his head.

"Down with thee, clod!" he shouted; and he showed such strength and fury that I scarce could look at the farmer, dreading to see his great head fly away. But just as the horse rushed at him, he leaped aside with most wonderful nimbleness, and the rider's sword was dashed out of his grasp, and down he went, over the back of the saddle, and his long legs spun up in the air, as a juggler tosses a two-pronged fork.

"Now for another!" the farmer cried, and his deep voice rang above the roar of Lynn; "or two at once, if it suits you better. I will teach you to carry off women, you dogs!"

But the outlaws would not try another charge. On a word from their leader they all dismounted, and were bringing their long guns to bear, and I heard the clink of their flints as they fixed the trigger. Carver Doone, grinding his enormous teeth, stood at the head of my horse, who was lashing and plunging, so that I must have been flung if any of the straps had given way. In terror of the gun flash I shut my eyes, for if I had seen that brave man killed, it would have been the death of me as well. Then I felt my horse treading on something soft. Carver Doone was beneath his feet, and an awful curse came from the earth.

"Have no fear!" said the sweetest voice that ever came into the ears of despair. "Sylvia, none can harm you now. Lie still, and let this protect your face."

"How can I help lying still?" I said, as a soft cloak was thrown over me, and in less than a moment my horse was rushing through branches and brushwood that swept his ears. At his side was another horse, and my bridle rein was held by a man who stooped over his neck in silence. Though his face was out of sight, I knew that Anthony Purvis was leading me.

There was no possibility of speaking now, but after a tumult of speed we came to an open glade where the trees fell back, and a gentle brook was gurgling. Then Captain Purvis cut my bonds, and lifting me down very softly, set me upon a bank of moss, for my limbs would not support me; and I lay there unable to do anything but weep.

When I returned to myself, the sun was just looking over a wooded cliff, and Anthony, holding a horn of water, and with water on his cheeks, was regarding me.

"Did you leave that brave man to be shot?" I asked, as if that were all my gratitude.

"I am not so bad as that," he answered, without any anger, for he saw that I was not in reason yet. "At sight of my men, although we were but five in all, the robbers fled, thinking the regiment was there; but it is God's truth that I thought little of anyone's peril compared with thine. But there need be no fear for John Ridd; the Doones are mighty afraid of him since he cast their culverin through their door."

"Was that the John Ridd I have heard so much of? Surely I might have known it, but my wits were shaken out of me."

"Yes, that was the mighty man of Exmoor, to whom thou owest more than life."

In horror of what I had so narrowly escaped, I fell upon my knees and thanked the Lord, and then I went shyly to the captain's side and said: "I am ashamed to look at thee. Without

Anthony Purvis, where should I be? Speak of no John Ridd to me."

For this man whom I had cast forth, with coldness, as he must have thought—although I knew better, when he was gone —this man (my honoured husband now, who hath restored me to my father's place, when kings had no gratitude or justice), Sir Anthony Purvis, as now he is, had dwelled in a hovel and lived on scraps, to guard the forsaken orphan, who had won, and shall ever retain, his love.

FRIDA; OR, THE LOVER'S LEAP.
A LEGEND OF THE WEST COUNTRY.
CHAPTER I.

On the very day when Charles I. was crowned with due rejoicings—Candlemas-day, in the year of our Lord 1626—a loyalty, quite as deep and perhaps even more lasting, was having its beer at Ley Manor in the north of Devon. A loyalty not to the king, for the old West-country folk knew little and cared less about the house that came over the Border; but to a lord who had won their hearts by dwelling among them, and dealing kindly, and paying his way every Saturday night. When this has been done for three generations general and genial respect may almost be relied upon. The present Baron de Wichehalse was fourth in descent from that Hugh de Wichehalse, the head of an old and wealthy race, who had sacrificed his comfort to his resolve to have a will of his own in matters of religion. That Hugh de Wichehalse, having an eye to this, as well as the other world, contrived to sell his large estates before they were confiscated, and to escape with all the money, from very sharp measures then enforced, by order of King Philip II., in the unhappy Low Countries. Landing in England, with all his effects and a score of trusty followers, he bought a fine property, settled, and died, and left a good name behind him. And that good name had been well kept up, and the property had increased and thriven, so that the present lord was loved and admired by all the neighbourhood.

In one thing, however, he had been unlucky, at least in his own opinion. Ten years of married life had not found issue in parental life. All his beautiful rocks and hills, lovely streams and glorious woods, green meadows and golden corn lands, must pass to his nephew and not to his child, because he had not gained one. Being a good man, he did his best to see this thing in its proper light. Children, after all, are a plague, a risk, and a deep anxiety. His nephew was a very worthy boy, and his rights should be respected. Nevertheless, the baron often longed to supersede them.

Of this there was every prospect now. The lady of the house had intrusted her case to a highly celebrated simple-woman, who lived among rocks and scanty vegetation at Heddon's Mouth, gathering wisdom from the earth and from the sea tranquillity. De Wichehalse was naturally vexed a little when all this accumulated wisdom culminated in nothing grander than a somewhat undersized, and unhappily female child—one, moreover, whose presence cost him that of his faithful and loving wife. So that the heiress of Ley Manor was greeted, after all, with a very brief and sorry welcome. "Jennyfried," for so they named her, soon began to grow into a fair esteem and good liking. Her father, after a year or two, plucked up his courage and played with her; and the more he played the more pleased he was, both with her and his own kind self. Unhappily, there were at that time no shops in the neighbourhood; unhappily, now there are too many. Nevertheless, upon the whole, she had all the toys that were good for her; and her teeth had a fair chance of fitting themselves for life's chief operation in the absence of sugared allurements.

A brief and meagre account is this of the birth, and growth, and condition of a maiden whose beauty and goodness still linger in the winter tales of many a simple homestead. For, sharing her father's genial nature, she went about among the people in her soft and playful way; knowing all their cares, and gifted with a kindly wonder at them, which is very soothing. All the simple folk expected condescension from her; and she would have let them have it, if she had possessed it.

At last she was come to a time of life when maidens really must begin to consider their responsibilities—a time when it does matter how the dress sits and what it is made of, and whether the hair is well arranged for dancing in the sunshine and for fluttering in the moonlight; also that the eyes convey not from that roguish nook the heart any betrayal of "hide and seek"; neither must the risk of blushing tremble on perpetual brinks; neither must—but, in a word, 'twas the seventeenth year of a maiden's life.

More and more such matters gained on her motherless necessity. Strictly anxious as she was to do the right thing always, she felt more and more upon every occasion (unless it was something particular) that her cousin need not so impress his cousinly salutation.

Albert de Wichehalse (who received that name before it became so inevitable) was that same worthy boy grown up as to whom the baron had felt compunctions, highly honourable to either party, touching his defeasance; or rather, perhaps, as to interception of his presumptive heirship by the said Albert, or at least by his mother contemplated. And Albert's father had entrusted him to his uncle's special care and love, having comfortably made up his mind, before he left this evil world, that his son should have a good slice of it.

Now, therefore, the baron's chief desire was to heal all breaches and make things pleasant, and to keep all the family property snug by marrying his fair Jennyfried (or "Frida," as she was called at home) to her cousin Albert, now a fine young fellow of five-and-twenty. De Wichehalse was strongly attached to his nephew, and failed to see any good reason why a certain large farm near Martinhoe, quite a huge cantle from the Ley estates, which by a prior devise must fall to Albert upon his own demise, should be allowed to depart in that way from his posthumous control.

However, like most of our fallible race, he went the worst possible way to work in pursuit of his favourite purpose. He threw the young people together daily, and dinned into the ears of each perpetual praise of the other. This seemed to answer well enough in the case of the simple Albert. He could never have too much of his lively cousin's company, neither could he weary of sounding her sweet excellence. But with the young maid it was not so. She liked the good Albert well enough, and never got out of his way at all. Moreover, sometimes his curly hair and bright moustache, when they came too near, would raise not a positive flutter, perhaps, but a sense of some fugitive movement in the unexplored distances of the heart. Still, this might go on for years, and nothing more to come of it. Frida loved her father best of all the world, at present.

CHAPTER II.

There happened to be at this time an old fogy—of course it is most distressing to speak of anyone disrespectfully; but when one thinks of the trouble he caused, and not only that, but he was an old fogy, essentially and pre-eminently—and his name was Sir Maunder Meddleby. This worthy baronet, one of the first of a newly invented order, came in his sled stuffed with goose-feathers (because he was too fat to ride, and no wheels were yet known on the hill tracks) to talk about some exchange of land with his old friend, our De Wichehalse. The baron and the baronet had been making a happy day of it. Each knew pretty well exactly what his neighbour's little rashness might be hoped to lead to, and each in his mind was pretty sure of having the upper hand of it. Therefore both their hearts were open—business being now dismissed, and dinner over—to one another. They sat in a beautiful place, and drew refreshment of mind through their outward lips by means of long reeden tubes with bowls at their ends, and something burning.

Clouds of delicate vapour wandered round and betwixt them and the sea; and each was well content to wonder whether the time need ever come when he must have to think again. Suddenly a light form flitted over the rocks, as the shadows flit; and though Frida ran away for fear of interrupting them, they knew who it was, and both, of course, began to think about her.

The baron gave a puff of his pipe, and left the baronet to begin. In course of time Sir Maunder spoke, with all that breadth and beauty of the vowels and the other things which a Devonshire man commands, from the lord lieutenant downward.

"If so be that 'ee gooth vor to ax me, ai can zay wan thing, and wan oney."

"What one thing is it, good neighbour? I am well content with her as she is."

"Laikely enough. And 'e wad be zo till 'e zeed a zummut fainer."

"I want to see nothing finer or better than what we have seen just now, sir."

"There, you be like all varthers, a'most! No zort o' oose to advaise 'un."

"Nay, nay! Far otherwise. I am not by any means of that nature. Sir Maunder Meddleby, I have the honour of craving your opinion."

Sir Maunder Meddleby thought for a while, or, at any rate, meant to be thinking, ere ever he dared to deliver himself of all his weighty judgment.

"I've a-knowed she, my Lord Witcher, ever since her wore that haigh. A purty wanch, and a peart one. But her wanteth the vinish of the coort. Never do no good wi'out un, whan a coomth, as her must, to coorting."

This was the very thing De Wichehalse was afraid to hear of. He had lived so mild a life among the folk who loved him that any fear of worry in great places was too much for him. And yet sometimes he could not help a little prick of thought about his duty to his daughter. Hence it came that common sense was driven wild by conscience, as forever happens with the few who keep that gadfly. Six great horses, who knew no conscience but had more fleshly tormentors, were ordered out, and the journey began, and at last it ended.

Everything in London now was going almost anyhow. Kind and worthy people scarcely knew the way to look at things. They desired to respect the king and all his privilege, and yet they found his mind so wayward that they had no hold of him.

The court, however, was doing its best, from place to place in its wanderings, to despise the uproar and enjoy itself as it used to do. Bright and beautiful ladies gathered round the king, when the queen was gone, persuading him and one another that they must have their own way.

Of the lords who helped these ladies to their strong

opinions there was none in higher favour with the queen and the king himself than the young Lord Auberley. His dress was like a sweet enchantment, and his tongue was finer still, and his grace and beauty were as if no earth existed. Frida was a new thing to him, in her pure simplicity. He to her was such a marvel, such a mirror of the skies, as a maid can only dream of in the full moon of St. John.

Little dainty glance, and flushing, and the fear to look too much, and the stealthy joy of feeling that there must be something meant, yet the terror of believing anything in earnest and the hope that, after all, there may be nought to come of it; and when this hope seems over true, the hollow of the heart behind it, and the longing to be at home with anyone to love oneself—time is wasted in recounting this that always must be.

Enough that Frida loved this gallant from the depths of her pure heart, while he admired and loved her to the best of his ability.

CHAPTER III.

The worthy baron was not of a versatile complexion. When his mind was quite made up he carried out the whole of it. But he could not now make up his mind upon either of two questions. Of these questions one was this—should he fight for the king or against him, in the struggle now begun? By hereditary instincts he was stanch for liberty, for letting people have their own opinions who could pay for them. And about religious matters and the royal view of them, he fell under sore misgiving that his grandfather on high would have a bone to pick with him.

His other difficulty was what to say, or what to think, about Lord Auberley. To his own plain way of judging, and that human instinct which, when highly cultivated, equals that of the weaker dogs, also to his recollection of what used to be expected in the time when he was young, Viscount Auberley did not give perfect satisfaction.

Nevertheless, being governed as strong folk are by the gentle ones, the worthy baron winked at little things which did not please him, and went so far as to ask that noble spark to flash upon the natives of benighted Devon. Lord Auberley was glad enough to retire for a season, both for other reasons and because he saw that bitter fighting must be soon expected. Hence it happened that the six great Flemish horses were buckled to, early in September of the first year of the civil war, while the king was on his westward march collecting men and money. The queen was not expected back from the Continent for another month; there had scarcely been for all the summer even the semblance of a court fit to teach a maiden lofty carriage and cold dignity; so that Lord de Wichehalse thought Sir Maunder Meddleby an oaf for sending him to London.

But there was someone who had tasted strong delight and shuddering fear, glowing hope and chill despair, triumph, shame, and all confusion of the heart and mind and will, such as simple maidens hug into their blushing chastity by the moonlight of first love. Frida de Wichehalse knew for certain, and forever felt it settled, that in all the world of worlds never had been any body, any mind, or even soul, fit to think of twice when once you had beheld Lord Auberley.

His young lordship, on the whole, was much of the same opinion. Low fellows must not have the honour to discharge their guns at him. He liked the king, and really meant no harm whatever to his peace of mind concerning his Henrietta; and, if the worst came to the worst, everyone knew that out of France there was no swordsman fit to meet, even with a rapier, the foil of Aubyn Auberley. Neither was it any slur upon his loyalty or courage that he was now going westward from the world of camps and war. It was important to secure the wavering De Wichehalse, the leading man of all the coast, from Minehead down to Hartland; so that, with the full consent of all the king's advisers, Lord Auberley left court and camp to press his own suit peacefully. What a difference he found it to be here in mid-September, far away from any knowledge of the world and every care; only to behold the manner of the trees disrobing, blushing with a trembling wonder at the freedom of the winds, or in the wealth of deep wood browning into rich defiance; only to observe the colour of the hills, and cliffs, and glens, and the glory of the sea underneath the peace of heaven, when the balanced sun was striking level light all over them! And if this were not enough to make a man contented with his littleness and largeness, then to see the freshened Pleiads, after their long dip of night, over the eastern waters twinkling, glad to see us all once more and sparkling to be counted.

These things, and a thousand others, which (without a waft of knowledge or of thought on our part) enter into and become our sweetest recollections, for the gay young lord possessed no charm, nor even interest. "Dull, dull, how dull it is!" was all he thought when he thought at all; and he vexed his host by asking how he could live in such a hole as that. And he would have vexed his young love, too, if young love were not so large of heart, by asking what the foreign tongue was which "her people" tried to speak. "Their native tongue and mine, my lord!" cried Frida, with the sweetness of her smile less true than usual, because she loved her people and the air of her nativity.

However, take it altogether, this was a golden time for her. Golden trust and reliance are the well-spring of our nature, and that man is the happiest who is cheated every day almost. The pleasure is tenfold as great in being cheated as to cheat. Therefore Frida was as happy as the day and night are long. Though the trees were striped with autumn, and the green of the fields was waning, and the puce of the heath was faded into dingy cinamon; though the tint of the rocks was darkened by the nightly rain and damp, and the clear brooks were beginning to be hoarse with shivering floods, and the only flowers left were but widows of the sun, yet she had the sovereign comfort and the cheer of trustful love. Lord Auberley, though he cared nought for the Valley of Rocks or Watersmeet, for beetling majesty of the cliffs or mantled curves of Woody Bay, and though he accounted the land a wilderness and the inhabitants savages, had taken a favourable view of the ample spread of the inland farms and the loyalty of the tenants, which naturally suggested the raising of the rental. Therefore he grew more attentive to young Mistress Frida; even sitting in shady places, which it made him damp to think of when he turned his eyes from her. Also he was moved a little by her growing beauty, for now the return to her native hills, the presence of her lover, and the home-made bread and forest mutton, combining with her dainty years, were making her look wonderful. If Aubyn Auberley had not been despoiled of all true manliness, by the petting and the forward wit of many a foreign lady, he might have won the pure salvation of an earnest love. But, when judged by that French standard which was now supreme at court, this poor Frida was a rustic, only fit to go to school.

There was another fine young fellow who thought wholly otherwise. To him, in his simple power of judging for himself, and seldom budging from that judgment, there was no one fit to dream of in comparison with her. Often, in this state of mind, he longed to come forward and let them know what he thought concerning the whole of it. But Albert could not see his way toward doing any good with it, and being of a bashful mind, he kept his heart in order.

CHAPTER IV.

The stir of the general rising of the kingdom against the king had not disturbed these places yet beyond what might be borne with. Everybody liked to talk, and everybody else was ready to put in a word or two; broken heads, however, were as yet the only issue. So that when there came great news of a real battle fought, and lost by Englishmen against Englishmen, the indignation of all the country ran against both parties.

Baron de Wichehalse had been thinking, after his crop of hay was in,—for such a faithful hay they have that it will not go from root to rick by less than two months of worrying,—from time to time, and even in the middle of his haycocks, this good lord had not been able to perceive his proper course. Arguments there were that sounded quite as if a baby must be perfectly convinced by them; and then there would be quite a different line of reason taken by someone who knew all about it and despised the opposite. So that many of a less decided way of thinking every day embraced whatever had been last confuted.

This most manly view of matters and desire to give fair play was scorned, of course, by the fairer (and unfairer) half of men. Frida counted all as traitors who opposed their liege the king.

"Go forth, my lord; go forth and fight," she cried to Viscount Auberley, when the doubtful combat of Edgehill was firing new pugnacity; "if I were a man, think you that I would let them do so?"

"Alas, fair mistress! it will take a many men to help it. But since you bid me thus away—hi, Dixon! get my trunks packed!" And then, of course, her blushing roses faded to a lily white; and then, of course, it was his duty to support her slender form; neither were those dulcet murmurs absent which forever must be present when the female kind begin to have the best of it.

So they went on once or twice, and would have gone on fifty times if fortune had allowed them thus to hang on one another. All the world was fair around them; and themselves, as fair as any, vouched the whole world to attest their everlasting constancy.

But one soft November evening, when the trees were full of drops, and gentle mists were creeping up the channels of the moorlands, and snipes (come home from foreign parts) were cheeping at their borings, and every weary man was gladdened by the glance of a bright wood fire, and smell of what was over it, there happened to come, on a jaded horse, a man, all hat, and cape, and boots, and mud, and sweat, and grumbling. All the people saw at once that it was quite impossible to make at all too much of him, because he must be full of news, which (after victuals) is the greatest need of human nature. So he had his own way as to everything he ordered; and, having ridden into much experience of women, kept himself as warm as could be, without any jealousy.

This stern man bore urgent order for the Viscount Auberley to join the king at once at Oxford, and bring with him all his gathering. Having gathered no men yet, but spent the time in plucking roses and the wild myrtles of Devonshire love, the young lord was for once a little taken aback at this order. Moreover, though he had been grumbling, half a dozen times a day—to make himself more precious—about the place, and the people, and the way they cooked his meals, he really meant it less and less as he came to know the neighbourhood. These are things which nobody can understand without seeing them.

"I grieve, my lord," said the worthy baron, "that you must leave us in this hot haste." On the whole, however, this excellent man was partly glad to be quit of him.

"And I am deeply indebted to your lordship for the grievance; but it must be so. *Que voulez-vous?* You talk the French, *mon baron?*"

"With a Frenchman, my lord; but not when I have the honour to speak with an Englishman."

"Ah, there! Foreign again! My lord, you will never speak English."

De Wichehalse could never be quite sure, though his race had been long in this country, whether he or they could speak born English as it ought to be.

"Perhaps you will find," he said at last, with grief as well as courtesy, "many who speak one language striving to silence one another."

"He fights best who fights the longest. You will come with us, my lord?"

"Not a foot, not half an inch," the baron answered sturdily. "I've a-laboured hard to zee my best, and 'a can't zee head nor tail to it."

Thus he spoke in imitation of what his leading tenant said, smiling brightly at himself, but sadly at his subject.

"Even so!" the young man answered; "I will forth and pay my duty. The rusty weathercock, my lord, is often too late for the oiling."

With this conceit he left De Wichehalse, and, while his grooms were making ready, sauntered down the zigzag path, which, through rocks and stubbed oaks, made toward the rugged headland known, far up and down the Channel, by the name of Duty Point. Near the end of this walk there lurked a soft and silent bower, made by Nature, and with all of Nature's art secluded. The ledge that wound along the rock-front widened, and the rock fell back and left a little cove, retiring into moss and ferny shade. Here the maid was well accustomed every day to sit and think, gazing down at the calm, gray sea, and filled with rich content and deep capacity of dreaming.

Here she was, at the present moment, resting in her pure love-dream, believing all the world as good, and true, and kind as her own young self. Round her all was calm and lovely; and the soft brown hand of autumn, with the sun's approval, tempered every mellow mood of leaves.

Aubyn Auberley was not of a sentimental cast of mind. He liked the poets of the day, whenever he deigned to read them; nor was he at all above accepting the dedication of a book. But it was not the fashion now—as had been in the noble time of Watson, Raleigh, and Shakspere—for men to look around and love the greater things they grow among.

Frida was surprised to see her dainty lord so early. She came here in the morning always, when it did not rain too hard, to let her mind have pasture on the landscape of sweet memory. And even sweeter hope was always fluttering in the distance, on the sea, or clouds, or flitting vapour of the morning. Even so she now was looking at the mounting glory of the sun above the sea-clouds, the sun that lay along the land, and made the distance roll away.

"Hard and bitter is my task," the gallant lord began with her, "to say farewell to all I love. But so it ever must be."

Frida looked at his riding-dress, and cold fear seized her suddenly, and then warm hope that he might only be riding after the bustards.

"My lord," she said, "will you never grant me that one little prayer of mine—to spare poor birds, and make those cruel gaze-hounds run down one another?"

"I shall never see the gaze-hounds more," he answered petulantly; "my time for sport is over. I must set forth for the war to-day."

"To-day!" she cried; and then tried to say a little more for pride's sake; "to go to the war to-day, my lord!"

"Alas! it is too true. Either I must go, or be a traitor and a dastard."

Her soft blue eyes lay full on his, and tears that had not time to flow began to spread a hazy veil between her and the one she loved.

He saw it, and he saw the rise and sinking of her wounded heart, and how the words she tried to utter fell away and died within her for the want of courage; and light and hard, and mainly selfish as his nature was, the strength, and depth, and truth of love came nigh to scare him for the moment even of his vanities.

"Frida!" he said, with her hand in his, and bending one knee on the moss; "only tell me that I must stay; then stay I will; the rest of the world may scorn if you approve me."

This, of course, sounded very well and pleased her, as it was meant to do; still, it did not satisfy her—so exacting are young maidens, and so keen is the ear of love.

"Aubyn, you are good and true. How very good and true you are! But even by your dear voice now I know what you are thinking."

Lord Auberley, by this time, was as well within himself again as he generally found himself; so that he began to balance chances very knowingly. If the king should win the warfare and be paramount again, this bright star of the court must rise to something infinitely higher than a Devonshire squire's child. A fine young widow of a duke, of the royal blood of France itself, was not far from being quite determined to accept him, if she only could be certain how these things would end themselves. Many other ladies were determined quite as bravely to wait the course of events, and let him have them, if convenient. On the other hand, if the kingdom should succeed in keeping the king in order—which was the utmost then intended—Aubyn Auberley might be only too glad to fall back upon Frida.

Thinking it wiser, upon the whole, to make sure of this little lamb, with nobler game in prospect, Lord Auberley heaved as deep a sigh as the size of his chest could compass. After which he spoke as follows, in a most delicious tone:

"Sweetest, and my only hope, the one star of my wanderings; although you send me forth to battle, where my arm is needed, give me one dear pledge that ever you will live and die my own."

This was just what Frida wanted, having trust (as our free-traders, by vast amplitude of vision, have in reciprocity) that if a man gets the best of a woman he is sure to give it back. Therefore these two sealed and delivered certain treaties (all unwritten, but forever engraven upon the best and tenderest feelings of the lofty human nature) that nothing less than death, or even greater, should divide them.

Is there one, among the many who survive such process, unable to imagine or remember how they parted? The fierce and even desperate anguish, nursed and made the most of; the pride and self-control that keep such things for comfort afterward; the falling of the heart that feels itself the true thing after all. Let it be so, since it must be; and no sympathy can heal it, since in every case it never, never, was so bad before!

CHAPTER V.

Lovers come, and lovers go; ecstasies of joy and anguish have their proper intervals; and good young folk, who know no better, revel in high misery. But the sun ascends the heavens at the same hour of the day, by himself dictated; and if we see him not, it is our earth that spreads the curtain. Nevertheless, these lovers, being out of rule with everything, heap their own faults on his head, and want him to be setting always, that they may behold the moon.

Therefore it was useless for the wisest man in the north of Devon, or even the wisest woman, to reason with young Frida now, or even to let her have the reason upon her side, and be sure of it. She, for her part, was astray from all the bounds of reason, soaring on the wings of faith, and hope, and high delusion. Though the winter-time was coming, and the wind was damp and raw, and the beauty of the valleys lay down to recover itself; yet with her the spring was breaking, and the world was lifting with the glory underneath it. Because it had been firmly pledged —and who could ever doubt it?—that the best and noblest lover in this world of noble love would come and grandly claim and win his bride on her next birthday.

At Christmas she had further pledge of her noble lover's constancy. In spite of difficulties, dangers, and the pressing need of men, he contrived to send her by some very valiant messengers (none of whom would ride alone) a beautiful portrait of himself, set round with sparkling diamonds; also a necklace of large pearls, as white and pure as the neck whose grace was to enhance their beauty.

Hereupon such pride and pleasure mounted into her cheeks and eyes, and flushed her with young gaiety, that all who loved her, being grafted with good superstition, nearly spoiled their Christmas-time by serious sagacity. She, however, in the wealth of all she had to think of, heeded none who trod the line of prudence and cold certainty.

"It is more than I can tell," she used to say, most prettily, to anybody who made bold to ask her about anything; "all things go so in and out that I am sure of nothing else except that I am happy."

The baron now began to take a narrow, perhaps a natural, view of all the things around him. In all the world there was for him no sign or semblance of any being whose desires or strictest rights could be thought of more than once when set against his daughter's. This, of course, was very bad for Frida's own improvement. It could not make her selfish yet, but it really made her wayward. The very best girls ever seen are sure to have their failings; and Frida, though one of the very best, was not above all nature. People made too much of this, when she could no more defend herself.

Whoever may have been to blame, one thing at least is certain—the father, though he could not follow all his child's precipitance, yet was well contented now to stoop his gray head to bright lips, and do his best toward believing some of their soft eloquence. The child, on the other hand, was full of pride, and rose on tiptoe, lest anybody might suppose her still too young for anything. Thus between them they looked forward to a pleasant time to come, hoping for the best, and judging everyone with charity.

The thing that vexed them most (for always there must, of course, be something) was the behaviour of Albert, nephew to the baron, and most loving cousin of Frida. Nothing they could do might bring him to spend his Christmas with them; and this would be the first time ever since his long-clothed babyhood that he had failed to be among them, and to lead or follow, just as might be required of him. Such a guest has no small value in a lonely neighbourhood, and years of usage mar the circle of the year without him.

Christmas passed, and New Year's Day, and so did many other days. The baron saw to his proper work, and took his turn of hunting, and entertained his neighbours, and pleased almost everybody. Much against his will, he had consented to the marriage of his daughter with Lord Auberley—to make the best of a bad job, as he told Sir Maunder Meddleby. Still, this kind and crafty father had his own ideas; for the moment he was swimming with the tide to please his daughter, even as for her dear sake he was ready to sink beneath it. Yet, these fathers have a right to form their own opinions; and for the most part they believe that they have more experience. Frida laughed at this, of course, and her father was glad to see her laugh. Nevertheless, he could not escape some respect for his own opinion, having so rarely found it wrong; and his own opinion was that something was very likely to happen.

In this he proved to be quite right. For many things began to happen, some on the right and some on the left hand of the baron's auguries. All of them, however, might be reconciled exactly with the very thing he had predicted. He noticed this, and it pleased him well, and inspired him so that he started anew for even truer prophecies. And everybody round the place was born so to respect him that, if he missed the mark a little, they could hit it for him.

Things stood thus at the old Ley Manor—and folk were content to have them so, for fear of getting worse, perhaps—toward the end of January, A. D. 1643. De Wichehalse had vowed that his only child—although so clever for her age, and prompt of mind and body—should not enter into marriage until she was in her eighteenth year. Otherwise, it would, no doubt, have all been settled long ago; for Aubyn Auberley sometimes had been in the greatest hurry. However, hither he must come now, as everybody argued, even though the fate of England hung on his stirrup-leather. Because he had even sent again, with his very best intentions, fashionable things for Frida, and the hottest messages; so that, if they did not mean him to be quite beside himself, everything must be smoking for his wedding at the

Candlemas.

But when everything and even everybody else—save Albert and the baron, and a few other obstinate people—was and were quite ready and rejoicing for a grand affair, to be celebrated with well-springs of wine and delightfully cordial Watersmeet, rocks of beef hewn into valleys, and conglomerate cliffs of pudding; when ruddy dame and rosy damsel were absorbed in "what to wear," and even steady farmers were in "practice for the back step"; in a word, when all the country was gone wild about Frida's wedding—one night there happened to come a man.

This man tied his horse to a gate and sneaked into the back yard, and listened in a quiet corner, knowing, as he did, the ins and outs and ways of the kitchen. Because he was that very same man who understood the women so, and made himself at home, by long experience, in new places. It had befallen this man, as it always befell any man of perception, to be smitten with the kindly loveliness of Frida. Therefore, now, although he was as hungry as ever he had been, his heart was such that he heard the sound of dishes, yet drew no nearer. Experience of human nature does not always spoil it.

CHAPTER VI.

When the baron at last received the letter which this rider had been so abashed to deliver, slow but lasting wrath began to gather in his gray-lashed eyes. It was the inborn anger of an honest man at villany mixed with lofty scorn and traversed by a dear anxiety. Withal he found himself so helpless that he scarce knew what to do. He had been to Frida both a father and a mother, as she often used to tell him when she wanted something; but now he felt that no man could administer the velvet touches of the female sympathy.

Moreover, although he was so kind, and had tried to think what his daughter thought, he found himself in a most ungenial mood for sweet condolement. Any but the best of fathers would have been delighted with the proof of all his prophecies and the riddance of a rogue. So that even he, though dwelling in his child's heart as his own, read this letter (when the first emotions had exploded) with a real hope that things, in the long run, would come round again.

"To my most esteemed and honoured friend, the Lord de Wichehalse, these from his most observant and most grateful Aubyn Auberley,—Under command of his Majesty, our most Royal Lord and King, I have this day been joined in bands of holy marriage with her Highness, the Duchess of B——, in France. At one time I had hope of favour with your good Lordship's daughter, neither could I have desired more complete promotion. But the service of the kingdom and the doubt of my own desert have forced me, in these troublous times, to forego mine own ambition. Our lord the King enjoins you with his Royal commendation, to bring your forces toward Bristowe by the day of St. Valentine. There shall I be in hope to meet your Lordship, and again find pleasure in such goodly company. Until then I am your Lordship's poor and humble servant,

"Aubyn Auberley."

Lord de Wichehalse made his mind up not to let his

daughter know until the following morning what a heavy blow had fallen on her faith and fealty. But, as evil chance would have it, the damsels of the house—and most of all the gentle cook-maid—could not but observe the rider's state of mind toward them. He managed to eat his supper in a dark state of parenthesis; but after that they plied him with some sentimental mixtures, and, being only a man at best, although a very trusty one, he could not help the rise of manly wrath at every tumbler. So, in spite of dry experience and careworn discretion, at last he let the woman know the whole of what himself knew. Nine good females crowded round him, and, of course, in their kind bosoms every word of all his story germinated ninety-fold.

Hence it came to pass that, after floods of tears in council and stronger language than had right to come from under aprons, Frida's nurse (the old herb-woman, now called "Mother Eyebright") was appointed to let her know that very night the whole of it. Because my lord might go on mooning for a month about it, betwixt his love of his daughter and his quiet way of taking things; and all that while the dresses might be cut, and trimmed, and fitted to a size and fashion all gone by before there came a wedding.

Mother Eyebright so was called both from the brightness of her eyes and her faith in that little simple flower, the euphrasia. Though her own love-tide was over, and the romance of life had long relapsed into the old allegiance to the hour of dinner, yet her heart was not grown tough to the troubles of the young ones; therefore all that she could do was done, but it was little.

Frida, being almost tired with the blissful cares of dress, happened to go up that evening earlier than her wont to bed. She sat by herself in the firelight, with many gorgeous things around her—wedding presents from great people, and (what touched her more) the humble offerings of her cottage friends. As she looked on these and thought of all the good will they expressed, and how a little kindness gathers such a heap of gratitude, glad tears shone in her bright eyes, and she only wished that all the world could be as blessed as she was.

To her entered Mother Eyebright, now unworthy of her name; and sobbing, writhing, crushing anguish is a thing which even Frida, simple and open-hearted one, would rather keep to her own poor self.

CHAPTER VII.

Upon the following day she was not half so wretched and lamentable as was expected of her. She even showed a brisk and pleasant air to the chief seamstress, and bade her keep some pretty things for the time of her own wedding. Even to her father she behaved as if there had been nothing more than happens every day. The worthy baron went to fold her in his arms, and let her cry there; but she only gave him a kiss, and asked the maid for some salt butter. Lord de Wichehalse, being disappointed of his outlet, thought (as all his life he had been forced to think continually) that any sort of woman, whether young or old, is wonderful. And so she carried on, and no one well could understand her.

She, however, in her own heart, knew the ups and downs of it. She alone could feel the want of any faith remaining, the ache of ever stretching forth and laying hold on nothing. Her mind had never been encouraged—as with maidens nowadays—to magnify itself, and soar, and scorn the heart that victuals it. All the deeper was her trouble, being less to be explained.

For a day or two the story is that she contrived to keep her distance, and her own opinion of what had been done to her. Child and almost baby as her father had considered her, even he was awed from asking what she meant to do about it. Something seemed to keep her back from speaking of her trouble, or bearing to have it spoken of. Only to her faithful hound, with whom she now began again to wander in the oak-wood, to him alone had she the comfort of declaring anything. This was a dog of fine old English breed and high connections, his great-grandmother having owned a kennel at Whitehall itself—a very large and well-conducted dog, and now an old one, going down into his grave without a stain upon him. Only he had shown such foul contempt of Aubyn Auberley, proceeding to extremes of ill-behaviour toward his raiment, that for months young Frida had been forced to keep him chained, and take her favourite walks without him.

"Ah, Lear!" now she cried, with sense of long injustice toward him; "you were right, and I was wrong; at least—at least it seems so."

"Lear," so called whether by some man who had heard of Shakspere, or (as seems more likely) from his peculiar way of contemplating the world at his own angle, shook his ears when thus addressed, and looked too wise for any dog to even sniff his wisdom.

Frida now allowed this dog to lead the way, and she would follow, careless of whatever mischief might be in the road for them. So he led her, without care or even thought on her part, to a hut upon the beach of Woody Bay; where Albert had set up his staff, to think of her and watch her. This, her cousin and true lover, had been grieving for her sorrow to the utmost power of a man who wanted her himself. It may have been beyond his power to help saying to himself sometimes, "How this serves her right, for making such a laughing-stock of me!" Nevertheless, he did his utmost to be truly sorrowful.

And now, as he came forth to meet her, in his fishing dress and boots (as different a figure as could be from Aubyn Auberley), memories of childish troubles and of strong protection thrilled her with a helpless hope of something to be done for her. So she looked at him, and let him see the state her eyes were in with constant crying, when there was not anyone to notice it. Also, she allowed him to be certain what her hands were like, and to be surprised how much she had fallen away in her figure. Neither was she quite as proud as might have been expected, to keep her voice from trembling or her plundered heart from sobbing. Only, let not anybody say a word to comfort her. Anything but that she now could bear, as she bore everything. It was, of course, the proper thing for everyone to scorn her. That, of course, she had fully earned, and met it, therefore, with disdain. Only, she could almost hate anybody who tried to comfort her.

Albert de Wichehalse, with a sudden start of intuition, saw what her father had been unable to descry or even dream. The worthy baron's time of life for fervid thoughts was over; for him despairing love was but a poet's fiction, or a joke against a pale young lady. But Albert felt from his own case, from burning jealousy suppressed, and cold neglect put up with, and all the other many-pointed aches of vain devotion, how sad must be the state of things when plighted faith was shattered also, and great ridicule left behind, with only a young girl to face it, motherless, and having none to stroke dishevelled hair, and coax the troubles by the firelight. However, this good fellow did the utmost he could do for her. Love and pity led him into dainty loving kindness; and when he could not find his way to say the right thing, he did better—he left her to say it. And so well did he move her courage, in his old protective way, without a word that could offend her or depreciate her love, that she for the moment, like a woman, wondered at her own despair. Also, like a woman, glancing into this and that, instead of any steadfast gazing, she had wholesome change of view, winning sudden insight into Albert's thoughts concerning her. Of course, she made up her mind at once, although her heart was aching so for want of any tenant, in a moment to extinguish any such presumption. Still, she would have liked to have it made a little clearer, if it were for nothing else than to be sure of something.

Albert saw her safely climb the steep and shaly walk that led, among retentive oak trees, or around the naked gully, all the way from his lonely cottage to the light, and warmth, and comfort of the peopled Manor House. And within himself he thought, the more from contrast of his own cold comfort and untended state:

"Ah! she will forget it soon; she is so young. She will soon get over that gay frippard's fickleness. To-morrow I will start upon my little errand cheerfully. After that she will come round; they cannot feel as we do."

Full of these fond hopes, he started on the following morning with set purpose to compel the man whom he had once disliked, and now despised unspeakably, to render some account of despite done to such a family. For, after all, the dainty viscount was the grandson of a goldsmith, who by brokerage for the Crown had earned the balls of his coronet. In quest of this gay fellow went the stern and solid Albert, leaving not a word about his purpose there behind him, but allowing everybody to believe what all found out. All found out, as he expected, that he was gone to sell his hay, perhaps as far as Taunton; and all the parish, looking forward to great rise of forage, felt indignant that he had not doubled his price, and let them think.

Alack-a-day and all the year round! that men perceive not how the women differ from them in the very source of thought. Albert never dreamed that his cousin, after doing so long without him, had now relapsed quite suddenly into her childish dependence upon him. And when she heard, on the following day, that he was gone for the lofty purpose of selling his seven ricks of hay, she said not a word, but only felt her cold heart so much colder.

CHAPTER VIII.

She had nothing now to do, and nobody to speak to; though her father did his utmost, in his kind and clumsy way, to draw his darling close to him. But she knew that all along he had disliked her idol, and she fancied, now and then, that this dislike had had something perhaps to do with what had befallen her. This, of course, was wrong on her part. But when youth and faith are wronged, the hurt is very apt to fly to all the tender places. Even the weather also seemed to have taken a turn against her. No wholesome frost set in to brace the slackened joints and make her walk until she began to tingle; neither was there any snow to spread a new cast on the rocks and gift the trees with airiness; nor even what mild winters, for the most part, bring in counterpoise—soft, obedient skies, and trembling pleasure of the air and earth. But—as over her own love—over all the country hung just enough of mist and chill to shut out cheerful prospect, and not enough to shut folk in to the hearth of their own comfort.

In her dull, forlorn condition, Frida still, through force of habit or the love of solitude, made her daily round of wood and rock, seashore and moorland. Things seemed to come across her now, instead of her going to them, and her spirit failed at every rise of the hilly road against her. In that dreary way she lingered, hoping nothing, fearing nothing, showing neither sigh nor tear, only seeking to go somewhere and be lost from self and sorrow in the cloudy and dark day.

Often thus the soft, low moaning of the sea encompassed her, where she stood, in forgotten beauty, careless of the wind and wave. The short, uneasy heave of waters in among the kelpy rocks, flowing from no swell or furrow on the misty glass of sea, but like a pulse of discontent, and longing to go further; after the turn, the little rattle of invaded pebbles, the lithe relapse and soft, shampooing lambency of oarweed, then the lavered boulders pouring gritty runnels back again, and every basined outlet wavering toward another inlet; these, and every phase of each innumerable to-and-fro, made or met their impress in her fluctuating misery.

"It is the only rest," she said; "the only chance of being quiet, after all that I have done, and all that people say of me."

None had been dastard enough to say a syllable against her; neither had she, in the warmest faith of love, forgotten truth; but her own dejection drove her, not to revile the world (as sour natures do consistently), but to shrink from sight, and fancy that the world was reviling her.

While she fluttered thus and hovered over the cold verge of death, with her sore distempered spirit, scarcely sure of anything, tidings came of another trouble, and turned the scale against her. Albert de Wichehalse, her trusty cousin and true lover, had fallen in a duel with that recreant and miscreant Lord Auberley. The strictest orders were given that this should be kept for the present from Frida's ears; but what is the use of the strictest orders when a widowed mother raves? Albert's mother vowed that "the shameless jilt" should hear it out, and slipped her guards and waylaid Frida on the morn of Candlemas, and overbore her with such words as may be well imagined.

"Auntie!" said the poor thing at last, shaking her beautiful curls, and laying one little hand to her empty heart, "don't be cross with me to-day. I am going home to be married, auntie. It is the day my Aubyn always fixed, and he never fails me."

"Little fool!" her aunt exclaimed, as Frida kissed her hand and courtesied, and ran round the corner; "one comfort is to know that she is as mad as a mole, at any rate."

CHAPTER IX.

Frida, knowing—perhaps more deeply than that violent woman thought—the mischief thus put into her, stole back to her bedroom, and, without a word to anyone, tired her hair in the Grecian snood which her lover used to admire so, and arrayed her soft and delicate form in all the bridal finery. Perhaps, that day, no bride in England—certainly none of her youth and beauty—treated her favourite looking-glass with such contempt and ingratitude. She did not care to examine herself, through some reluctant sense of havoc, and a bitter fear that someone might be disappointed in her. Then at the last, when all was ready, she snatched up her lover's portrait (which for days had been cast aside and cold), and, laying it on her bosom, took a snatch of a glance at her lovely self.

After some wonder she fetched a deep sigh—not from clearly thinking anything, but as an act of nature—and said, "Good-by!" forever, with a little smile of irony, to her looking-glass, and all the many pretty things that knew her.

It was her bad luck, as some people thought thereafter—or her good luck, as herself beheld it—to get down the stairs and out of the house without anyone being the wiser. For the widow De Wichehalse, Albert's mother, had not been content with sealing the doom of this poor maiden, but in that highly excited state, which was to be expected, hurried into the house, to beard the worthy baron in his den. There she found him; and, although he said and did all sympathy, the strain of parental feelings could not yield without "hysterics."

All the servants, and especially Mother Eyebright (whose chief duty now was to watch Frida), were called by the terrified baron, and with one unanimous rush replied; so that the daughter of the house left it without notice, and before any glances was out of sight, in the rough ground where the deer were feeding, and the umber oak-leaves hung.

It was the dainty time when first the year begins to have a

little hope of meaning kindly—when in the quiet places often, free from any haste of wind, or hindrances of pattering thaw, small and unimportant flowers have a little knack of dreaming that the world expects them. Therefore neither do they wait for leaves to introduce them, nor much weather to encourage, but in shelfy corners come, in a day, or in a night—no man knows quite which it is; and there they are, as if by magic, asking, "Am I welcome?" And if anybody sees them, he is sure to answer "Yes."

Frida, in the sheltered corners and the sunny nooks of rock, saw a few of these little things delicately trespassing upon the petulance of spring. Also, though her troubles wrapped her with an icy mantle, softer breath of Nature came, and sighed for her to listen to it, and to make the best of all that is not past the sighing. More than once she stopped to listen, in the hush of the timid south wind creeping through the dishevelled wood; and once, but only once, she was glad to see her first primrose and last, and stooped to pluck, but, on second thoughts, left it to outblossom her.

So, past many a briered rock, and dingle buff with littered fern, green holly copse where lurked the woodcock, and arcades of zigzag oak, Frida kept her bridal robe from spot, or rent, or blemish. Passing all these little pleadings of the life she had always loved, at last she turned the craggy corner into the ledge of the windy cliff.

Now below her there was nothing but repose from shallow thought; rest from all the little troubles she had made so much of; deep, eternal satisfaction in the arms of something vast. But all the same, she did not feel quite ready for the great jump yet.

The tide was in, and she must wait at least until it began to turn, otherwise her white satin velvet would have all its pile set wrong, if ever anybody found her. There could be no worse luck than that for any bride on her wedding-day; therefore up the rock-walk Frida kept very close to the landward side.

All this way she thought of pretty little things said to her in the early days of love. Many things that made her smile because they had gone so otherwise, and one or two that would have fetched her tears, if she had any. Filled with vain remembrance thus, and counting up the many presents sent to her for this occasion, but remaining safe at home, Frida came to the little coving bower just inside the Point, where she could go no further. Here she had received the pledges, and the plight, and honour; and here her light head led her on to look for something faithful.

"When the tide turns I shall know it. If he does not come by that time, there will be no more to do. It will be too late for weddings, for the tide turns at twelve o'clock. How calm and peaceful is the sea! How happy are the sea gulls, and how true to one another!"

She stood where, if she had cared for life, it would have been certain death to stand, so giddy was the height, and the rock beneath her feet so slippery. The craggy headland, Duty Point, well known to every navigator of that rock-bound coast, commands the Channel for many a league, facing eastward the Castle Rock and Countisbury Foreland, and westward Highveer Point, across the secluded cove of Leymouth. With one sheer fall of a hundred fathoms the stern cliff meets the baffled sea—or met it then, but now the level of the tide is lowering. Air and sea were still and quiet; the murmur of the multitudinous wavelets could not climb the cliff; but loops and curves of snowy braiding on the dark gray water showed the set of tide and shift of current in and out the buried rocks.

Standing in the void of fear, and gazing into the deep of death, Frida loved the pair of sea gulls hovering halfway between her and the soft gray sea. These good birds had found a place well suited for their nesting, and sweetly screamed to one another that it was a contract. Frida watched how proud they were, and how they kept their strong wings sailing and their gray backs flat and quivering, while with buoyant bosom each made circles round the other.

As she watched, she saw the turning of the tide below them. The streaky bends of curdled water, lately true as fairy-rings, stopped and wavered, and drew inward on their flowing curves, and outward on the side toward the ebb. Then the south wind brought the distant toll of her father's turret-clock, striking noon with slow deliberation and dead certainty.

Frida made one little turn toward her bower behind the cliff, where the many sweet words spoken drew her to this last of hope. All was silent. There was no one. Now was the time to go home at last.

Suddenly she felt a heavy drag upon her velvet skirt. Ancient Lear had escaped from the chain she had put on him, and, more trusty than mankind, was come to keep his faith with her.

"You fine old dog, it is too late! The clock has struck. The tide has turned. There is no one left to care for me; and I have ruined everyone. Good-by, you only true one!"

Submissive as he always was, the ancient dog lay down when touched, and drew his grizzled eyelids meekly over his dim and sunken eyes. Before he lifted them again Frida was below the sea gulls, and beneath the waves they fished.

Lear, with a puzzled sniff, arose and shook his head, and peered, with his old eyes full of wistful wonder, down the fearful precipice. Seeing something, he made his mind up, gave one long re-echoed howl, then tossed his mane, like a tawny wave, and followed down the death-leap.

Neither body was ever found; and the whole of this might not have been known so clearly as it is known, unless it had happened that Mother Eyebright, growing uneasy, came round the corner just in time to be too late. She, like a sensible woman, never dreamed of jumping after them, but ran home so fast that she could not walk to church for three months afterward; and when her breath came back was enabled to tell tenfold of all she had seen.

* * * * *

One of the strangest things in life is the way in which we mortals take the great and fatal blows of life.

For instance, the baron was suddenly told, while waiting for Frida to sit beside him, at his one o'clock dinner:

"Plaize, my lard, your lardship's darter hath a been and jumped off Duty Point."

"What an undutiful thing to do!" was the first thing Lord de Wichehalse said; and those who knew no better thought that this was how he took it.

Aubyn Auberley, however, took a different measure of a broken-hearted father's strength. For the baron buckled on the armour of a century ago, which had served his grandsire through hard blows in foreign battles, and, with a few of his trusty servants, rode to join the Parliament. It happened so that he could not make redress of his ruined life until the middle of the summer. Then, at last, his chance came to him, and he did not waste it. Viscount Auberley, who had so often slipped away and laughed at him, was brought to bay beneath a tree in the famous fight of Lansdowne.

The young man offered to hold parley, but the old man had no words. His snowy hair and rugged forehead, hard-set mouth and lifted arm, were enough to show his meaning. The gallant, being so skilled of fence, thought to play with this old man as he had with his daughter; but the Gueldres ax cleft his curly head, and split what little brain it takes to fool a trusting maiden.

So, in early life, deceiver and deceived were quit of harm; and may ere now have both found out whether it is better to inflict the wrong or suffer it.

GEORGE BOWRING.
A TALE OF CADER IDRIS.
CHAPTER I.

When I was a young man, and full of spirits, some forty years ago or more, I lost my best and truest friend in a very sad and mysterious way. The greater part of my life has been darkened by this heavy blow and loss, and the blame which I poured upon myself for my own share in the matter.

George Bowring had been seven years with me at the fine old school of Shrewsbury, and trod on my heels from form to form so closely that, when I became at last the captain of the school, he was second to me. I was his elder by half a year, and "sapped" very hard, while he laboured little; so that it will be plain at a glance, although he never acknowledged it, that he was the better endowed of the two with natural ability. At that time we of Salop always expected to carry everything, so far as pure scholarship was concerned, at both the universities. But nowadays I am grieved to see that schools of quite a different stamp (such as Rugby and Harrow, and even Marlborough, and worse of all peddling Manchester) have been running our boys hard, and sometimes almost beating them. And how have they done it? Why, by purchasing masters of our prime rank and special style.

George and myself were at one time likely, and pretty well relied upon, to keep up the fame of Sabrina's crown, and hold our own at Oxford. But suddenly it so fell out that both of us were cut short of classics, and flung into this unclassic world. In the course of our last half year at school and when we were both taking final polish to stand for Balliol scholarships, which we were almost sure to win, as all the examiners were Shrewsbury men,—not that they would be partial to us, but because we knew all their questions,—within a week, both George and I were forced to leave the dear old school, the grand old town, the lovely Severn, and everything but one another.

He lost his father; I lost my uncle, a gentleman in Derbyshire, who had well provided my education; but, having a family of his own, could not be expected to leave me much. And he left me even less than could, from his own point of view, have been rational. It is true that he had seven children; but still a man of £15,000 a year might have done, without injustice—or, I might say, with better justice—something more than to leave his nephew a sum which, after much pushing about into divers insecurities, fetched £72 10s. per annum.

Nevertheless, I am truly grateful; though, perhaps, at the time I had not that knowledge of the world which enlarges the grateful organs. It cannot matter what my feelings were, and I never was mercenary. All my sentiments at that period ran in Greek senarii; and perhaps it would show how good and lofty boys were in that ancient time, though now they are only rude Solecists, if I were to set these verses down—but, after much consideration, I find it wiser to keep them in.

George Bowring's father had some appointment well up in the Treasury. He seems to have been at some time knighted for finding a manuscript of great value that went in the end to the paper mills. How he did it, or what it was, or whether he ever did it at all, were questions for no one to meddle with. People in those days had larger minds than they ever seem to exhibit now. The king might tap a man, and say, "Rise, Sir Joseph," and all the journals of the age, or, at least, the next day, would echo "Sir Joseph!" And really he was worthy of it. A knight he lived, and a knight he died; and his widow found it such a comfort!

And now on his father's sudden death, George Bowring was left not so very well off. Sir Joseph had lived, as a knight should do, in a free-handed, errant, and chivalrous style; and what he left behind him made it lucky that the title dropped. George, however, was better placed, as regards the world, than I was; but not so very much as to make a difference between us. Having always held together, and being started in life together, we resolved to face the world (as other people are always called) side by side, and with a friendship that should make us as good as one.

This, however, did not come out exactly as it should have done. Many things arose between us—such as diverse occupation, different hours of work and food, and a little split in the taste of trowsers, which, of course, should not have been. He liked the selvage down his legs, while I thought it unartistic, and, going much into the graphic line, I pressed my objections strongly.

But George, in the handsomest manner—as now, looking back on the case, I acknowledge—waived my objections, and insisted as little as he could upon his own. And again we became as tolerant as any two men, at all alike, can be of one another.

He, by some postern of influence, got into some dry ditch of the Treasury, and there, as in an old castle-moat, began to be at home, and move, gently and after his seniors, as the young ducks follow the old ones. And at every waddle he got more money.

My fortune, however, was not so nice. I had not Sir Joseph, of Treasury cellars, to light me with his name and memory into a snug cell of my own. I had nothing to look to but courage, and youth, and education, and three-quarters of a hundred pounds a year, with some little change to give out of it. Yet why should I have doubted? Now, I wonder at my own misgivings; yet all of them still return upon me, if I ever am persuaded just to try Welsh rabbit. Enough, that I got on at last, to such an extent that the man at the dairy offered me half a year's milk for a sketch of a cow that had never belonged to him.

George, meanwhile, having something better than a brush for a walking stick and an easel to sit down upon, had taken unto himself a wife—a lady as sweet and bright as could be—by name Emily Atkinson. In truth, she was such a charming person that I myself, in a quiet way, had taken a very great fancy to her before George Bowring saw her; but as soon as I found what a desperate state the heart of poor George was reduced to, and came to remember that he was fitted by money to marry, while I was not, it appeared to me my true duty toward the young lady and him, and even myself, to withdraw from the field, and have nothing to say if they set up their horses together.

So George married Emily, and could not imagine why it was that I strove in vain to appear as his "best man," at the rails where they do it.

For though I had ordered a blue coat and buttons, and a cashmere waistcoat (amber-coloured, with a braid of peonies), yet at the last moment my courage failed me, and I was caught with a shivering in the knees, which the doctor said was ague. This and that shyness of dining at his house (which I thought it expedient to adopt during the years of his married life) created some little reserve between us, though hardly so bad as our first disagreement concerning the stripe down the pantaloons.

However, before that dereliction I had made my friend a wedding present, as was right and proper—a present such as nothing less than a glorious windfall could have enabled me to buy. For while engaged, some three years back, upon a grand historical painting of "Cœur de Lion and Saladin," now to be seen—but let that pass; posterity will always know where to find it—I was harassed in mind perpetually concerning the grain of the fur of a cat. To the dashing young artists of the present day this may seem a trifle; to them, no doubt, a cat is a cat—or would be, if they could make it one. Of course, there are cats enough in London, and sometimes even a few to spare; but I wanted a cat of peculiar order, and of a Saracenic cast. I walked miles and miles; till at last I found him residing in a very old-fashioned house in the Polygon, at Somers Town. Here was a genuine paradise of cats, carefully ministered to and guarded by a maiden lady of Portuguese birth and of advanced maturity. Each of these nine cats possessed his own stool—a mahogany stool, with a velvet cushion, and his name embroidered upon it in beautiful letters of gold. And every day they sat round the fire to digest their dinners, all nine of them, each on his proper stool, some purring, some washing their faces, and some blinking or nodding drowsily. But I need not have spoken of this, except that one of them was called "Saladin." He was the very cat I wanted. I made his acquaintance in the area, and followed it up on the knife-boy's board. And then I had the most happy privilege of saving him from a tail-pipe. Thus my entrance was secured into this feline Eden; and the lady was so well pleased that she gave me an order for nine full-length cat portraits, at the handsome price of ten guineas apiece. And not only this, but at her demise—which followed, alas! too speedily—she left me £150, as a proof of her esteem and affection.

This sum I divided into three equal parts—fifty pounds for a present for George, another fifty for a duty to myself, and the residue to be put by for any future purposes. I knew that my friend had no gold watch; neither, of course, did I possess one. In those days a gold watch was thought a good deal of, and made an impression in society, as a three-hundred-guinea ring does now. Barwise was then considered the best watchmaker in London, and perhaps in the world. So I went to his shop, and chose two gold watches of good size and substance—none of your trumpery catchpenny things, the size of a gilt pill trodden upon —at the price of fifty guineas each. As I took the pair, the foreman let me have them for a hundred pounds, including also in that figure a handsome gold key for each, of exactly the same pattern, and a guard for the fob of watered black-silk ribbon.

My reason for choosing these two watches, out of a trayful of similar quality, was perhaps a little whimsical—viz., that the numbers they bore happened to be sequents. Each had its number engraved on its white enamel dial, in small but very clear figures, placed a little above the central spindle; also upon the extreme verge, at the nadir below the seconds hand, the name of the maker, "Barwise, London." They were not what are called "hunting watches," but had strong and very clear lunette glasses fixed in rims of substantial gold. And their respective numbers were 7777 and 7778.

Carrying these in wash-leather bags, I gave George Bowring his choice of the two; and he chose the one with four figures of seven, making some little joke about it, not good enough to repeat, nor even bad enough to laugh at.

CHAPTER II.

For six years after this all went smoothly with George Bowring and myself. We met almost daily, although we did not lodge together (as once we had done) nor spend the evening hours together, because, of course, he had now his home and family rising around him. By the summer of 1832 he had three children, and was expecting a fourth at no very distant time. His eldest son was named after me, "Robert Bistre," for such is my name, which I have often thought of changing. Not that the name is at all a bad one, as among friends and relations, but that, when I am addressed by strangers, "Mr. Bistre" has a jingling sound, suggestive of childish levity. "Sir Robert Bistre," however, would sound uncommonly well; and (as some people say) less eminent artists—but perhaps, after all, I am not so very old as to be in a hurry.

In the summer of 1832—as elderly people will call to mind, and the younger sort will have heard or read—the cholera broke over London like a bursting meteor. Such panic had not been known, I believe, since the time of the plague, in the reign of Charles II., as painted (beyond any skill of the brush) by the simple and wonderful pen of Defoe. There had been in the interval many seasons—or at least I am informed so—of sickness more widely spread, and of death more frequent, if not so sudden. But now this new plague, attacking so harshly a man's most perceptive and valued part, drove rich people out of London faster than horses (not being attacked) could fly. Well, used as I was to a good deal of poison in dealing with my colours, I felt no alarm on my own account, but was anxious about my landlady. This was an excellently honest woman of fifty-five summers at the utmost, but weakly confessing to as much as forty. She had made a point of insisting upon a brisket of beef and a flat-polled cabbage for dinner every Saturday; and the same, with a "cowcumber," cold on Sunday; and for supper a soft-roed herring, ever since her widowhood.

"Mrs. Whitehead," said I—for that was her name, though she said she did not deserve it; and her hair confirmed her in that position by growing darker from year to year—"Madam, allow me to beg you to vary your diet a little at this sad time."

"I varies it every day, Mr. Bistre," she answered somewhat snappishly. "The days of the week is not so many but what they all come round again."

For the moment I did not quite perceive the precision of her argument; but after her death I was able to do more justice to her intellect. And, unhappily, she was removed to a better world on the following Sunday.

To a man in London of quiet habits and regular ways and periods there scarcely can be a more desperate blow than the loss of his landlady. It is not only that his conscience pricks him for all his narrow, plagiaristic, and even irrational suspicions about the low level of his tea caddy, or a neap tide in his brandy bottle, or any false evidence of the eyes (which ever go spying to lock up the heart), or the ears, which are also wicked organs—these memories truly are grievous to him, and make him yearn now to be robbed again; but what he feels most sadly is the desolation of having nobody who understands his locks. One of the best men I ever knew was so plagued with his sideboard every day for two years, after dinner, that he married a little new maid-of-all-work —because she was a blacksmith's daughter.

Nothing of that sort, however, occurred in my case, I am proud to say. But finding myself in a helpless state, without anyone to be afraid of, I had only two courses before me: either to go back to my former landlady (who was almost too much of a Tartar, perhaps), or else to run away from my rooms till Providence provided a new landlady.

Now, in this dilemma I met George Bowring, who saw my distress, and most kindly pressed me to stay at his house till some female arose to manage my affairs for me. This, of course, I declined to do, especially under present circumstances; and, with mutual pity, we parted. But the very next day he sought me out, in a quiet nook where a few good artists were accustomed to meet and think; and there he told me that really now he saw his way to cut short my troubles as well as his own, and to earn a piece of enjoyment and profit for both of us. And I happen to remember his very words.

"You are cramped in your hand, my dear fellow," said he (for in those days youths did not call each other "old man"— with sad sense of their own decrepitude). "Bob, you are losing your freedom of touch. You must come out of these stony holes, and look at a rocky mountain."

My heart gave a jump at these words; and yet I had been too much laid flat by facts—"sat upon," is the slang of these last twenty years, and in the present dearth of invention must serve, no doubt, for another twenty—I say that I had been used as a cushion by so many landladies and maids-of-all-work (who take not an hour to find out where they need do no work), that I could not fetch my breath to think of ever going up a mountain.

"I will leave you to think of it, Bob," said George, putting his hat on carefully; "I am bound for time, and you seem to be nervous. Consult your pillow, my dear fellow; and peep into your old stocking and see whether you can afford it."

That last hit settled me. People said, in spite of all my generous acts—and nobody knows, except myself, the frequency and the extent of these—without understanding the merits of the case—perfect (or rather imperfect) strangers said that I was stingy! To prove the contrary, I resolved to launch into great expenditure, and to pay coach fare all the way from London toward the nearest mountain.

Half the inhabitants now were rushing helter-skelter out of London, and very often to seaside towns where the smell of fish destroyed them. And those who could not get away were shuddering at the blinds drawn down, and huddling away from the mutes at the doors, and turning pale at the funeral bells. And some, who had never thought twice before of their latter end, now began to dwell with so much unction upon it, that Providence graciously spared them the waste of perpetual preparation.

Among the rest, George Bowring had been scared, far more than he liked to own, by the sudden death of his butcher, between half a dozen chops for cutlets and the trimming of a wing-bone. George's own cook had gone down with the order, and meant to bring it all back herself, because she knew what butchers do when left to consider their subject. And Mrs. Tompkins was so alarmed that she gave only six hours' notice to leave, though her husband was far on the salt-sea wave, according to her own account, and she had none to make her welcome except her father's second wife. This broke up the household; and hence it was that George tempted me so with the mountains.

For he took his wife and children to an old manor-house in Berkshire, belonging to two maiden aunts of the lady, who promised to see to all that might happen, but wanted no gentleman in the house at a period of such delicacy. George Bowring, therefore, agreed to meet me on the 12th day of September, at the inn in Reading—I forget its name—where the Regulator coach (belonging to the old company, and leaving White Horse Cellars at half-past nine in the morning) allowed an hour to dine, from one o'clock onward, as the roads might be. And here I found him, and we supped at Oxford, and did very well at the Mitre. On the following morning we took coach for Shrewsbury, as we had agreed, and, reaching the town before dark, put up at the Talbot Inn, and sauntered into the dear old school, to see what the lads had been at since our time; for their names and their exploits, at Oxford and Cambridge, are scored in large letters upon the panels, from the year 1806 and onward, so that soon there will be no place to register any more of them; and we found that though we ourselves had done nothing, many fine fellows had been instituted in letters of higher humanity, and were holding up the old standard, so that we longed to invite them to dinner. But discipline must be maintained; and that word means, more than anything else, the difference of men's ages.

Now, at Shrewsbury, we had resolved to cast off all further heed of coaches; and knowing the country pretty well, or recalling it from our childhood, to strike away on foot for some of the mountain wildernesses. Of these, in those days, nobody knew much more than that they were high and steep, and slippery and dangerous, and much to be shunned by all sensible people who liked a nice fire and the right side of the window. So that when we shouldered staves with knapsacks flapping heavily, all the wiser sort looked on us as marching off to Bedlam.

In the morning, as we were starting, we set our watches by the old school dial, as I have cause to remember well. And we staked half a crown, in a sporting manner, each on his own watch to be the truer by sun upon our way back again. And thus we left those ancient walls and the glancing of the river, and stoutly took the Welshpool road, dreading nought except starvation.

Although in those days I was not by any means a cripple, George was far stronger of arm and leg, having always been famous, though we made no fuss about such things then, for running and jumping, and lifting weights, and using the boxing-gloves and the foils. A fine, brave fellow as ever lived, with a short, straight nose and a resolute chin, he touched the measuring-bar quite fairly at seventy-four inches, and turned the scales at fourteen stone and a quarter. And so, as my chattels weighed more than his (by means of a rough old easel and material for rude sketches), he did me a good turn now and then by changing packs for a mile or two. And thus we came in four days' march to Aber-Aydyr, a village lying under Cader Idris.

CHAPTER III.

If any place ever lay out of the world, and was proud of itself for doing so, this little village of Aber-Aydyr must have been very near it. The village was built, as the people expressed it, of thirty cottages, one public-house, one shop universal, and two chapels. The torrent of the Aydyr entered with a roar of rapids, and at the lower end departed in a thunder of cascades. The natives were all so accustomed to live in the thick of this watery uproar that, whenever they left their beloved village to see the inferior outer world, they found themselves as deaf as posts till they came to a weir or a waterfall. And they told us that in the scorching summer of the year 1826 the river had failed them so that for nearly a month they could only discourse by signs; and they used to stand on the bridge and point at the shrunken rapids, and stop their ears to exclude that horrible emptiness. Till a violent thunderstorm broke up the drought, and the river came down roaring; and the next day all Aber-Aydyr was able to gossip again as usual.

Finding these people, who lived altogether upon slate, of a quaint and original turn, George Bowring and I resolved to halt and rest the soles of our feet a little, and sketch and fish the neighbourhood. For George had brought his rod and tackle, and many a time had he wanted to stop and set up his rod and begin to cast; but I said that I would not be cheated so: he had promised me a mountain, and would he put me off with a river? Here, however, we had both delights; the river for him and the mountain for me. As for the fishing, all that he might have, and I would grudge him none of it, if he fairly divided whatever he caught. But he must not expect me to follow him always and watch all his dainty manœuvring; each was to carry and eat his own dinner, whenever we made a day of it, so that he might keep to his flies and his water, while I worked away with my brush at the mountains. And thus we spent a most pleasant week, though we knew very little of Welsh and the slaters spoke but little

English. But—much as they are maligned because they will not have strangers to work with them—we found them a thoroughly civil, obliging, and rather intelligent set of men; most of them also of a respectable and religious turn of mind; and they scarcely ever poach, except on Saturdays and Mondays.

On September 25, as we sat at breakfast in the little sanded parlour of the Cross-Pipes public house, our bedroom being overhead, my dear friend complained to me that he was tired of fishing so long up and down one valley, and asked me to come with him further up, into wilder and rockier districts, where the water ran deeper (as he had been told) and the trout were less worried by quarrymen, because it was such a savage place, deserted by all except evil spirits, that even the Aber-Aydyr slaters could not enjoy the fishing there. I promised him gladly to come, only keeping the old understanding between us, that each should attend to his own pursuits and his own opportunities mainly; so that George might stir most when the trout rose well, and I when the shadows fell properly. And thus we set forth about nine o'clock of a bright and cheerful morning, while the sun, like a courtly perruquier of the reign of George II., was lifting, and shifting, and setting in order the vapoury curls of the mountains.

We trudged along thus at a merry swing, for the freshness of autumnal dew was sparkling in the valley, until we came to a rocky pass, where walking turned to clambering. After an hour of sharpish work among slaty shelves and threatening crags, we got into one of those troughlike hollows hung on each side with precipices, which look as if the earth had sunk for the sake of letting the water through. On our left hand, cliff towered over cliff to the grand height of Pen y Cader, the steepest and most formidable aspect of the mountain. Rock piled on rock, and shingle cast in naked waste disdainfully, and slippery channels scooped by torrents of tempestuous waters, forbade one to desire at all to have anything more to do with them—except, of course, to get them painted at a proper distance, so that they might hang at last in the dining rooms of London, to give people appetite with sense of hungry breezes, and to make them comfortable with the sight of danger.

"This is very grand indeed," said George, as he turned to watch me; for the worst part of our business is to have to give an opinion always upon points of scenery. But I am glad that I was not cross, or even crisp with him that day.

"It is magnificent," I answered; "and I see a piece of soft sward there, where you can set up your rod, old fellow, while I get my sticks in trim. Let us fill our pipes and watch the shadows; they do not fall quite to suit me yet."

"How these things make one think," cried Bowring, as we sat on a stone and smoked, "of the miserable littleness of men like you and me, Bob!"

"Speak for yourself, sir," I said, laughing at his unaccustomed, but by no means novel, reflection. "I am quite contented with my size, although I am smaller than you, George. Dissatisfied mortal! Nature wants no increase of us, or she would have had it."

"In another world we shall be much larger," he said, with his eyes on the tops of the hills. "Last night I dreamed that my wife and children were running to meet me in heaven, Bob."

"Tush! You go and catch fish," I replied; for tears were in his large, soft eyes, and I hated the sentimental. "Would they ever let such a little Turk as Bob Bistre into heaven, do you think? My godson would shout all the angels deaf and outdrum all the cherubim."

"Poor little chap! He is very noisy; but he is not half a bad sort," said George. "If he only comes like his godfather I shall wish no better luck for him."

These were kind words, and I shook his hand to let him know that I felt them; and then, as if he were ashamed of having talked rather weakly, he took with his strong legs a dangerous leap of some ten or twelve feet downward, and landed on a narrow ledge that overhung the river. Here he put his rod together, and I heard the click of reel as he drew the loop at the end of the line through the rings, and so on; and I heard him cry "Chut!" as he took his flies from his Scotch cap and found a tangle; and I saw the glistening of his rod, as the sunshine pierced the valley, and then his tall, straight figure pass the corner of a crag that stood as upright as a tombstone; and after that no more of any live and bright George Bowring.

CHAPTER IV.

Swift is the flight of Time whenever a man would fain lay hold of him. All created beings, from Behemoth to a butterfly, dread and fly (as best they may) that universal butcher—man. And as nothing is more carefully killed by the upper sort of mankind than Time, how can he help making off for his life when anybody wants to catch him?

Of course, I am not of that upper sort, and make no pretence to be so; but Time, perhaps, may be excused for thinking—having had such a very short turn at my clothes—that I belonged to the aristocracy. At any rate, while I drew, and rubbed, and dubbed, and made hieroglyphics, Time was uneasily shifting and shuffling the lines of the hills, as a fever patient jerks and works the bed-clothes. And, worse than that, he was scurrying westward (frightened, no doubt, by the equinox) at such a pace that I was scared by the huddling together of shadows. Awaking from a long, long dream—through which I had been working hard, and laying the foundations of a thousand pounds hereafter—I felt the invisible damp of evening settling in the valleys. The sun, from over the sea, had still his hand on Cader Idris; but every inferior head and height was gray in the sweep of his mantle.

I threw my hair back—for an artist really should be picturesque; and, having no other beauty, must be firm to long hair, while it lasts—and then I shouted, "George!" until the strata of the mountain (which dip and jag, like veins of oak) began and sluggishly prolonged a slow zigzag of echoes. No counter-echo came to me; no ring of any sonorous voice made crag, and precipice, and mountain vocal with the sound of "Bob!"

"He must have gone back. What a fool I must be never to remember seeing him! He saw that I was full of rubbish, and he would not disturb me. He is gone back to the Cross-Pipes, no doubt. And yet it does not seem like him."

"To look for a pin in a bundle of hay" would be a job of

sense and wisdom rather than to seek a thing so very small as a very big man among the depth, and height, and breadth of river, shingle, stone, and rock, crag, precipice, and mountain. And so I doubled up my things, while the very noise they made in doubling flurried and alarmed me; and I thought it was not like George to leave me to find my way back all alone, among the deep bogs, and the whirlpools, and the trackless tracts of crag.

When I had got my fardel ready, and was about to shoulder it, the sound of brisk, short steps, set sharply upon doubtful footing, struck my ear, through the roar of the banks and stones that shook with waterfall. And before I had time to ask, "Who goes there?"—as in this solitude one might do—a slight, short man, whom I knew by sight as a workman of Aber-Aydyr, named Evan Peters, was close to me, and was swinging a slate-hammer in one hand, and bore in the other a five-foot staff. He seemed to be amazed at sight of me, but touched his hat with his staff, and said: "Good-night, gentleman!" in Welsh; for the natives of this part are very polite. "Good-night, Evan!" I answered, in his own language, of which I had picked up a little; and he looked well pleased, and said in his English: "For why, sir, did you leave your things in that place there? A bad mans come and steal them, it is very likely."

Then he wished me "Good-night" again, and was gone—for he seemed to be in a dreadful hurry—before I had the sense to ask him what he meant about "my things." But as his footfall died away a sudden fear came over me.

"The things he meant must be George Bowring's," I said to myself; and I dropped my own, and set off, with my blood all tingling, for the place toward which he had jerked his staff. How long it took me to force my way among rugged rocks and stubs of oak I cannot tell, for every moment was an hour to me. But a streak of sunset glanced along the lonesome gorge, and cast my shadow further than my voice would go; and by it I saw something long and slender against a scar of rock, and standing far in front of me. Toward this I ran as fast as ever my trembling legs would carry me, for I knew too well that it must be the fishing-rod of George Bowring.

It was stuck in the ground—not carelessly, nor even in any hurry; but as a sportsman makes all snug, when for a time he leaves off casting. For instance, the end fly was fixed in the lowest ring of the butt, and the slack of the line reeled up so that the collar lay close to the rod itself. Moreover, in such a rocky place, a bed to receive the spike could not have been found without some searching. For a moment I was reassured. Most likely George himself was near—perhaps in quest of blueberries (which abound at the foot of the shingles and are a very delicious fruit), or of some rare fern to send his wife, who was one of the first in England to take much notice of them. And it shows what confidence I had in my friend's activity and strength, that I never feared the likely chance of his falling from some precipice.

But just as I began, with some impatience—for we were to have dined at the Cross-Pipes about sundown, five good (or very bad) miles away, and a brace of ducks was the order—just as I began to shout, "George! Wherever have you got to?" leaping on a little rock, I saw a thing that stopped me. At the further side of this rock, and below my feet, was a fishing basket, and a half-pint mug nearly full of beer, and a crust of the brown, sweet bread of the hills, and a young white onion, half cut through, and a clasp-knife open, and a screw of salt, and a slice of the cheese, just dashed with goat's milk, which George was so fond of, but I disliked; and there may have been a hard-boiled egg. At the sight of these things all my blood rushed to my head in such a manner that all my power to think was gone. I sat down on the rock where George must have sat while beginning his frugal luncheon, and I put my heels into the marks of his, and, without knowing why, I began to sob like a child who has lost his mother. What train of reasoning went through my brain—if any passed in the obscurity—let metaphysicians or psychologists, as they call themselves, pretend to know. I only know that I kept on whispering, "George is dead! Unless he had been killed, he never would have left his beer so!"

I must have sat, making a fool of myself, a considerable time in this way, thinking of George's poor wife and children, and wondering what would become of them, instead of setting to work at once to know what was become of him. I took up a piece of cheese-rind, showing a perfect impression of his fine front teeth, and I put it in my pocketbook, as the last thing he had touched. And then I examined the place all around and knelt to look for footmarks, though the light was sadly waning.

For the moment I discovered nothing of footsteps or other traces to frighten or to comfort me. A little narrow channel (all of rock and stone and slaty stuff) sloped to the river's brink, which was not more than five yards distant. In this channel I saw no mark except that some of the smaller stones appeared to have been turned over; and then I looked into the river itself, and saw a force of water sliding smoothly into a rocky pool.

"If he had fallen in there," I said, "he would have leaped out again in two seconds; or even if the force of the water had carried him down into that deep pool, he can swim like a duck — of course he can. What river could ever drown you, George?"

And then I remembered how at Salop he used to swim the flooded Severn when most of us feared to approach the banks; and I knew that he could not be drowned, unless something first had stunned him. And after that I looked around, and my heart was full of terror.

"It is a murder!" I cried aloud, though my voice among the rocks might well have brought like fate upon me. "As sure as I stand here, and God is looking down upon me, this is a black murder!"

In what way I got back that night to Aber-Aydyr I know not. All I remember is that the people would not come out of their houses to me, according to some superstition, which was not explained till morning; and, being unable to go to bed, I took a blanket and lay down beneath a dry arch of the bridge, and the Aydyr, as swiftly as a spectre gliding, hushed me with a melancholy song.

CHAPTER V.

Now, as sure as ever I lay beneath the third arch of Aber-Aydyr Bridge, in a blanket of Welsh serge or flannel, with a double border, so surely did I see, and not dream, what I am going to tell you.

The river ran from east to west; and the moon, being now the harvest moon, was not very high, but large and full, and just gliding over the crest of the hill that overhangs the quarry-pit; so that, if I can put it plainly, the moon was across the river from me, and striking the turbulent water athwart, so that her face, or a glimmer thereof, must have been lying upon the river if any smooth place had been left for it. But of this there was no chance, because the whole of the river was in a rush, according to its habit, and covered with bubbles, and froth, and furrows, even where it did not splash, and spout, and leap, as it loved to do. In the depth of the night, when even the roar of the water seemed drowsy and indolent, and the calm trees stooped with their heavy limbs overhanging the darkness languidly, and only a few rays of the moon, like the fluttering of a silver bird, moved in and out the mesh-work, I leaned upon my elbow, and I saw the dead George Bowring.

He came from the pit of the river toward me, quietly and without stride or step, gliding over the water like a mist or the vapour of a calm white frost; and he stopped at the ripple where the shore began, and he looked at me very peacefully. And I felt neither fear nor doubt of him, any more than I do of this pen in my hand.

"George," I said, "I have been uneasy all the day about you and I cannot sleep, and I have had no comfort. What has made you treat me so?"

He seemed to be anxious to explain, having always been so straightforward; but an unknown hand or the power of death held him, so that he could only smile. And then it appeared to me as if he pointed to the water first and then to the sky, with such an import that I understood (as plainly as if he had pronounced it) that his body lay under the one and his soul was soaring on high through the other; and, being forbidden to speak, he spread his hands, as if entrusting me with all that had belonged to him; and then he smiled once more, and faded into the whiteness of the froth and foam.

And then I knew that I had been holding converse, face to face, with Death; and icy fear shook me, and I strove in vain to hide my eyes from everything. And when I awoke in the morning there was a gray trunk of an alder tree, just George Bowring's height and size, on the other side of the water, so that I could have no doubt that himself had been there.

After a search of about three hours we found the body of my dear friend in a deep black pool of the Aydyr—not the first hole below the place in which he sat down to his luncheon, but nearly a hundred yards farther down, where a bold cliff jutted out and bent the water scornfully. Our quarrymen would not search this pool until the sunlight fell on it, because it was a place of dread with a legend hovering over it. "The Giant's Tombstone" was the name of the crag that overhung it; and the story was that the giant Idris, when he grew worn out with age, chose this rock out of many others near the top of the mountain, and laid it under his arm and came down here to drink of the Aydyr. He drank the Aydyr dry because he was feverish and flushed with age; and he set down the crag in a hole he had scooped with the palms of his hands for more water; and then he lay down on his back, and Death (who never could reach to his knee when he stood) took advantage of his posture to drive home the javelin. And thus he lay dead, with the crag for his headstone, and the weight of his corpse sank a grave for itself in the channel of the river, and the toes of his boots are still to be seen after less than a mile of the valley.

Under this headstone of Idris lay the body of George Bowring, fair and comely, with the clothes all perfect, and even the light cap still on the head. And as we laid it upon the grass, reverently and carefully, the face, although it could smile no more, still appeared to wear a smile, as if the new world were its home, and death a mere trouble left far behind. Even the eyes were open, and their expression was not of fright or pain, but pleasant and bright, with a look of interest such as a man pays to his food.

"Stand back, all of you!" I said sternly; "none shall examine him but myself. Now all of you note what I find here."

I searched all his pockets, one after another; and tears came to my eyes again as I counted not less than eleven of them, for I thought of the fuss we used to make with the Shrewsbury tailor about them. There was something in every pocket, but nothing of any importance at present, except his purse and a letter from his wife, for which he had walked to Dolgelly and back on the last entire day of his life.

"It is a hopeless mystery!" I exclaimed aloud, as the Welshmen gazed with superstitious awe and doubt. "He is dead as if struck by lightning, but there was no storm in the valley!"

"No, no, sure enough; no storm was there. But it is plain to see what has killed him!" This was Evan Peters, the quarryman, and I glanced at him very suspiciously. "Iss, sure, plain enough," said another; and then they all broke into Welsh, with much gesticulation; and "e-ah, e-ah," and "otty, otty," and "hanool, hanool," were the sounds they made—at least to an ignorant English ear.

"What do you mean, you fools?" I asked, being vexed at their offhand way of settling things so far beyond them. "Can you pretend to say what it was?"

"Indeed, then, and indeed, my gentleman, it is no use to talk no more. It was the Caroline Morgan."

"Which is the nearest house?" I asked, for I saw that some of them were already girding up their loins to fly, at the mere sound of that fearful name; for the cholera morbus had scared the whole country; and if one were to fly, all the rest would follow, as swiftly as mountain sheep go. "Be quick to the nearest house, my friends, and we will send for the doctor."

This was a lucky hit; for these Cambrians never believed in anyone's death until he had "taken the doctor." And so, with much courage and kindness, "to give the poor gentleman the last chance," they made a rude litter, and, bearing the body upon sturdy shoulders, betook themselves to a track which I had overlooked entirely. Some people have all their wits about them as soon as they are called for, but with me it is mainly otherwise. And this I had shown in two things already; the first of which came to my mind the moment I pulled out my watch to see what the time was. "Good Heavens!" it struck me, "where is George's watch? It was not in any of his pockets; and I did not feel it in his fob."

In an instant I made them set down the bier; and, much as it grieved me to do such a thing, I carefully sought for my dear friend's watch. No watch, no seals, no ribbon, was there! "Go on," I said; and I fell behind them, having much to think about. In this condition, I took little heed of the distance, or of the ground itself; being even astonished when, at last, we stopped; as if we were bound to go on forever.

CHAPTER VI.

We had stopped at the gate of an old farmhouse, built with massive boulder stones, laid dry, and flushed in with mortar. As dreary a place as was ever seen; at the head of a narrow mountain-gorge, with mountains towering over it. There was no sign of life about it, except that a gaunt hog trotted forth, and grunted at us, and showed his tusks, and would perhaps have charged us, if we had not been so many. The house looked just like a low church-tower, and might have been taken for one at a distance if there had been any battlements. It seemed to be four or five hundred years old, and perhaps belonged to some petty chief in the days of Owen Glendower.

"Knock again, Thomas Edwards. Stop, let me knock," said one of our party impatiently. "There, waddow, waddow, waddow!"

Suiting the action to the word, he thumped with a big stone heavily, till a middle-aged woman, with rough black hair, looked out of a window and screamed in Welsh to ask what this terrible noise was. To this they made answer in the same language, pointing to their sad burden, and asking permission to leave it for the doctor's inspection and the inquest, if there was to be one. And I told them to add that I would pay well—anything, whatever she might like to ask. But she screamed out something that sounded like a curse, and closed the lattice violently. Knowing that many superstitions lingered in these mountains— as, indeed, they do elsewhere plentifully—I was not surprised at the woman's stern refusal to admit us, especially at this time of pest; but I thought it strange that her fierce black eyes avoided both me and the poor rude litter on which the body of George lay, covered with some slate-workers' aprons.

"She is not the mistress!" cried Evan Peters, in great excitement, as I thought. "Ask where is Hopkin—Black Hopkin —where is he?"

At this suggestion a general outcry arose in Welsh for

"Black Hopkin"; an outcry so loud and prolonged that the woman opened the window again and screamed—as they told me afterward—"He is not at home, you noisy fools; he is gone to Machynlleth. Not long would you dare to make this noise if Hopkin ap Howel was at home."

But while she was speaking the wicket-door of the great arched gate was thrown open, and a gun about six feet long and of very large bore was presented at us. The quarrymen drew aside briskly, and I was about to move somewhat hastily, when the great, swarthy man who was holding the gun withdrew it, and lifted his hat to me, proudly and as an equal.

"You cannot enter this house," he said in very good English, and by no means rudely. "I am sorry for it, but it cannot be. My little daughter is very ill, the last of seven. You must go elsewhere."

With these words he bowed again to me, while his sad eyes seemed to pierce my soul; and then he quietly closed the wicket and fastened it with a heavy bolt, and I knew that we must indeed go further.

This was no easy thing to do; for our useless walk to "Crug y Dlwlith" (the Dewless Hills), as this farm was called, had taken us further at every step from the place we must strive for after all—the good little Aber-Aydyr. The gallant quarrymen were now growing both weary and uneasy; and in justice to them I must say that no temptation of money, nor even any appeal to their sympathies, but only a challenge of their patriotism held them to the sad duties owing from the living to the dead. But knowing how proud all Welshmen are of the fame of their race and country, happily I exclaimed at last, when fear was getting the mastery, "What will be said of this in England, this low cowardice of the Cymro?" Upon that they looked at one another and did their best right gallantly.

Now, I need not go into any further sad details of this most sad time, except to say that Dr. Jones, who came the next day from Dolgelly, made a brief examination by order of the coroner. Of course, he had too much sense to suppose that the case was one of cholera; but to my surprise he pronounced that death was the result of "asphyxia, caused by too long immersion in the water." And knowing nothing of George Bowring's activity, vigour, and cultivated power in the water, perhaps he was not to be blamed for dreaming that a little mountain stream could drown him. I, on the other hand, felt as sure that my dear friend was foully murdered as I did that I should meet him in heaven—if I lived well for the rest of my life, which I resolved at once to do—and there have the whole thing explained, and perhaps be permitted to glance at the man who did it, as Lazarus did at Dives.

In spite of the doctor's evidence and the coroner's own persuasion, the jury found that "George Bowring died of the Caroline Morgan"—which the clerk corrected to cholera morbus —"brought on by wetting his feet and eating too many fish of his own catching." And so you may see it entered now in the records of the court of the coroners of the king for Merioneth.

And now I was occupied with a trouble, which, after all, was more urgent than the enquiry how it came to pass. When a man is dead, it must be taken as a done thing, not to be undone; and, happily, all near relatives are inclined to see it in that light. They are grieved, of course, and they put on hatbands and give no dinner parties; and they even think of their latter ends more than they might have desired to do. But after a little while all comes round. Such things must be happening always, and it seems so unchristian to repine; and if any money has been left them, truly they must attend to it. On the other hand, if there has been no money, they scarcely see why they should mourn for nothing; and, as a duty, they begin to allow themselves to be roused up.

But when a wife becomes a widow, it is wholly different. No money can ever make up to her the utter loss of the love-time and the loneliness of the remaining years; the little turns, and thoughts, and touches—wherever she goes and whatever she does—which at every corner meet her with a deep, perpetual want. She tries to fetch her spirit up and to think of her duties to all around—to her children, or to the guests whom trouble forces upon her for business' sake, or even the friends who call to comfort (though the call can fetch her none); but all the while how deeply aches her sense that all these duties are as different as a thing can be from her love-work to her husband!

What could I do? I had heard from George, but could not for my life remember, the name of that old house in Berkshire where poor Mrs. Bowring was on a visit to two of her aunts, as I said before. I ventured to open her letter to her husband, found in his left-hand side breast-pocket, and, having dried it, endeavoured only to make out whence she wrote; but there was nothing. Ladies scarcely ever date a letter both with time and place, for they seem to think that everybody must know it, because they do. So the best I could do was to write to poor George's house in London, and beg that the letter might be forwarded at once. It came, however, too late to hand. For, although the newspapers of that time were respectably slow and steady, compared with the rush they all make nowadays, they generally managed to outrun the post, especially in the nutting season. They told me at Dolgelly, and they confirmed it at Machynlleth, that nobody must desire to get his letters at any particular time, in the months of September and October, when the nuts were ripe. For the postmen never would come along until they had filled their bags with nuts, for the pleasure of their families. And I dare say they do the same thing now, but without being free to declare it so.

CHAPTER VII.

The body of my dear friend was borne round the mountain slopes to Dolgelly and buried there, with no relative near, nor any mourner except myself; for his wife, or rather his widow, was taken with sudden illness (as might be expected), and for weeks it was doubtful whether she would stay behind to mourn for him. But youth and strength at last restored her to dreary duties and worldly troubles.

Of the latter, a great part fell on me; and I did my best—though you might not think so, after the fuss I made of my own—to intercept all that I could, and quit myself manfully of the trust which George had returned from the dead to enjoin. And, what with one thing and another, and a sudden dearth of money which fell on me (when my cat-fund was all spent, and my gold watch gone up a gargoyle), I had such a job to feed the living that I never was able to follow up the dead.

The magistrates held some enquiry, of course, and I had to give my evidence; but nothing came of it, except that the quarryman, Evan Peters, clearly proved his innocence. Being a very clever fellow, and dabbling a bit in geology, he had taken his hammer up the mountains, as his practice was when he could spare the time, to seek for new veins of slate, or lead, or even gold, which is said to be there. He was able to show that he had been at Tal y Llyn at the time of day when George would be having his luncheon; and the people who knew Evan Peters were much more inclined to suspect me than him. But why should they suspect anybody, when anyone but a fool could see "how plain it was of the cholera?"

Twenty years slipped by (like a rope paid out on the seashore, "hand over hand," chafing as it goes, but gone as soon as one looks after it), and my hair was gray, and my fame was growing (slowly, as it appeared to me, but as all my friends said "rapidly"; as if I could never have earned it!) when the mystery of George Bowring's death was solved without an effort.

I had been so taken up with the three dear children, and working for them as hard as if they were my own (for the treasury of our British empire was bankrupt to these little ones —"no provision had been made for such a case," and so we had to make it)—I say that these children had grown to me and I to them in such degree that they all of them called me "Uncle!"

This is the most endearing word that one human being can use to another. A fellow is certain to fight with his brothers and sisters, his father, and perhaps even his mother. Tenfold thus with his wife; but whoever did fight with his uncle? Of course I mean unless he was his heir. And the tenderness of this relation has not escaped *vox populi*, that keen discriminator. Who is the most reliable, cordial, indispensable of mankind—especially to artists—in every sense of the word the dearest? A pawnbroker; he is our uncle.

Under my care, these three children grew to be splendid "members of society." They used to come and kick over my easel with legs that were quite Titanic; and I could not scold them when I thought of George. Bob Bistre, the eldest, was my apprentice, and must become famous in consequence; and when he was twenty-five years old, and money became no object to me (through the purchase by a great art critic of the very worst picture I ever painted; half of it, in fact, was Bob's!), I gave the boy choice of our autumn trip to California, or the antipodes.

"I would rather go to North Wales, dear uncle," he answered, and then dropped his eyes, as his father used when he had provoked me. That settled the matter. He must have his way; though as for myself, I must confess that I have begun, for a long time now, upon principle, to shun melancholy.

The whole of the district is opened up so by those desperate railways that we positively dined at the Cross-Pipes Hotel the very day after we left Euston Square. Our landlady did not remember me, which was anything but flattering. But she jumped at Bob as if she would have kissed him; for he was the image of his father, whose handsome face had charmed her.

CHAPTER VIII.

The Aydyr was making as much noise as ever, for the summer had been a wet one; and of course all the people of Aber-Aydyr had their ears wide open. I showed Bob the bridge and the place of my vision, but did not explain its meaning, lest my love for him should seem fiduciary; and the next morning, at his most urgent request, we started afoot for that dark, sad valley. It was a long walk, and I did not find that twenty years had shortened it.

"Here we are at last," I said, "and the place looks the same as ever. There is the grand old Pen y Cader, with the white cloud rolling as usual; to the left and right are the two other summits, the arms of the chair of Idris; and over the shoulder of that crag you can catch a glassy light in the air—that is the reflection of Tal y Llyn."

"Yes, yes!" he answered impatiently. "I know all that from your picture, uncle. But show me the place where my father died."

"It lies immediately under our feet. You see that gray stone down in the hollow, a few yards from the river brink. There he sat, as I have often told you, twenty years ago this day. There he was taking his food, when someone——Well, well! God knows, but we never shall. My boy, I am stiff in the knees; go on."

He went on alone, as I wished him to do, with exactly his father's step, and glance, figure, face, and stature. Even his dress was of the silver-gray which his father had been so fond of, and which the kind young fellow chose to please his widowed mother. I could almost believe (as a cloudy mantle stole in long folds over the highland, reproducing the lights, and shades, and gloom of that mysterious day) that the twenty years were all a dream, and that here was poor George Bowring going to his murder and his watery grave.

My nerves are good and strong, I trow; and that much

must have long been evident. But I did not know what young Bob's might be, and therefore I left him to himself. No man should be watched as he stands at the grave of his wife or mother: neither should a young fellow who sits on the spot where his father was murdered. Therefore, as soon as our Bob had descended into the gray stone-pit, in which his dear father must have breathed his last, I took good care to be out of sight, after observing that he sat down exactly as his father must have sat, except that his attitude, of course, was sad, and his face pale and reproachful. Then, leaving the poor young fellow to his thoughts, I also sat down to collect myself.

But before I had time to do more than wonder at the mysterious ways of the world, or of Providence in guiding it; at the manner in which great wrong lies hidden, and great woe falls unrecompensed; at the dark, uncertain laws which cover (like an indiscriminate mountain cloud) the good and the bad, the kind and the cruel, the murdered and the murderer—a loud shriek rang through the rocky ravine, and up the dark folds of the mountain.

I started with terror, and rushed forward, and heard myself called, and saw young Bowring leap up, and stand erect and firm, although with a gesture of horror. At his feet lay the body of a man struck dead, flung on its back, with great hands spread on the eyes, and white hair over them.

No need to ask what it meant. At last the justice of God was manifest. The murderer lay, a rigid corpse, before the son of the murdered.

"Did you strike him?" I asked.

"Is it likely," said the youth, "that I would strike an aged man like that? I assure you I never had such a fright in my life. This poor old fellow came on me quite suddenly, from behind a rock, when all my mind was full of my father; and his eyes met mine, and down he fell, as if I had shot him through the heart!"

"You have done no less," I answered; and then I stooped

over the corpse (as I had stooped over the corpse of its victim), and the whole of my strength was required to draw the great knotted hands from the eyes, upon which they were cramped with a spasm not yet relaxed.

"It is Hopkin ap Howel!" I cried, as the great eyes, glaring with the horror of death, stood forth. "Black Hopkin once, white Hopkin now! Robert Bowring, you have slain the man who slew your father."

"You know that I never meant to do it," said Bob. "Surely, uncle, it was his own fault!"

"How did he come? I see no way. He was not here when I showed you the place, or else we must have seen him."

"He came round the corner of that rock, that stands in front of the furze-bush."

Now that we had the clue, a little examination showed the track. Behind the furze-bush, a natural tunnel of rock, not more than a few yards long, led into a narrow gorge covered with brushwood, and winding into the valley below the farmhouse of the Dewless Crags. Thither we hurried to obtain assistance, and there the whole mystery was explained.

Black Hopkin (who stole behind George Bowring and stunned, or, perhaps, slew him with one vile blow) has this and this only to say at the Bar—that he did it through love of his daughter.

Gwenthlian, the last of seven, lay dying on the day when my friend and myself came up the valley of the Aydyr. Her father, a man of enormous power of will and passion, as well as muscle, rushed forth of the house like a madman, when the doctor from Dolgelly told him that nothing more remained except to await the good time of heaven. It was the same deadly decline which had slain every one of his children at that same age, and now must extinguish a long descended and slowly impoverished family.

"If I had but a gold watch I could save her!" he cried in

his agony, as he left the house. "Ever since the old gold watch was sold, they have died—they have died! They are gone, one after one, the last of all my children!"

In these lonely valleys lurks a strange old superstition that even Death must listen to the voice of Time in gold; that, when the scanty numbered moments of the sick are fleeting, a gold watch laid in the wasted palm, and pointing the earthly hours, compels the scythe of Death to pause, the timeless power to bow before the two great gods of the human race—time and gold.

Poor George in the valley must have shown his watch. The despairing father must have been struck with crafty madness at the sight. The watch was placed in his daughter's palm; but Death had no regard for it. Thenceforth Black Hopkin was a blasted man, racked with remorse and heart-disease, sometimes raving, always roving, but finding no place of repentance. And it must have been a happy stroke—if he had made his peace above, which none of us can deal with—when the throb of his long-worn heart stood still at the vision of his victim, and his soul took flight to realms that have no gold and no chronometer.

CROCKER'S HOLE.
PART I.

The Culm, which rises in Somersetshire, and hastening into a fairer land (as the border waters wisely do) falls into the Exe near Killerton, formerly was a lovely trout stream, such as perverts the Devonshire angler from due respect toward Father Thames and the other canals round London. In the Devonshire valleys it is sweet to see how soon a spring becomes a rill, and a rill runs on into a rivulet, and a rivulet swells into a brook; and before one has time to say, "What are you at?"—before the first tree it ever spoke to is a dummy, or the first hill it ever ran down has turned blue, here we have all the airs and graces, demands and assertions of a full-grown river.

But what is the test of a river? Who shall say? "The power to drown a man," replies the river darkly. But rudeness is not argument. Rather shall we say that the power to work a good undershot wheel, without being dammed up all night in a pond, and leaving a tidy back-stream to spare at the bottom of the orchard, is a fair certificate of riverhood. If so, many Devonshire streams attain that rank within five miles of their spring; aye, and rapidly add to it. At every turn they gather aid, from ash-clad dingle and aldered meadow, mossy rock and ferny wall, hedge-trough roofed with bramble netting, where the baby water lurks, and lanes that coming down to ford bring suicidal tribute. Arrogant, all-engrossing river, now it has claimed a great valley of its own; and whatever falls within the hill scoop, sooner or later belongs to itself. Even the crystal "shutt" that crosses the farmyard by the woodrick, and glides down an aqueduct of last year's bark for Mary to fill the kettle from; and even the tricklets that have no organs for telling or knowing their business, but only get into unwary oozings in and among the water-grass, and there make moss and forget themselves among it—one and all, they come to the same thing at last, and that is the river.

The Culm used to be a good river at Culmstock,

tormented already by a factory, but not strangled as yet by a railroad. How it is now the present writer does not know, and is afraid to ask, having heard of a vile "Culm Valley Line." But Culmstock bridge was a very pretty place to stand and contemplate the ways of trout; which is easier work than to catch them. When I was just big enough to peep above the rim, or to lie upon it with one leg inside for fear of tumbling over, what a mighty river it used to seem, for it takes a treat there and spreads itself. Above the bridge the factory stream falls in again, having done its business, and washing its hands in the innocent half that has strayed down the meadows. Then under the arches they both rejoice and come to a slide of about two feet, and make a short, wide pool below, and indulge themselves in perhaps two islands, through which a little river always magnifies itself, and maintains a mysterious middle. But after that, all of it used to come together, and make off in one body for the meadows, intent upon nurturing trout with rapid stickles, and buttercuppy corners where fat flies may tumble in. And here you may find in the very first meadow, or at any rate you might have found, forty years ago, the celebrated "Crocker's Hole."

The story of Crocker is unknown to me, and interesting as it doubtless was, I do not deal with him, but with his Hole. Tradition said that he was a baker's boy who, during his basket-rounds, fell in love with a maiden who received the cottage-loaf, or perhaps good "Households," for her master's use. No doubt she was charming, as a girl should be, but whether she encouraged the youthful baker and then betrayed him with false rôle, or whether she "consisted" throughout,—as our cousins across the water express it,—is known to their *manes* only. Enough that she would not have the floury lad; and that he, after giving in his books and money, sought an untimely grave among the trout. And this was the first pool below the bread-walk deep enough to drown a five-foot baker boy. Sad it was; but such things must be, and bread must still be delivered daily.

A truce to such reflections,—as our foremost writers always say, when they do not see how to go on with them,—but it is a serious thing to know what Crocker's Hole was like; because at a time when (if he had only persevered, and married the maid, and succeeded to the oven, and reared a large family of short-weight bakers) he might have been leaning on his crutch beside the pool, and teaching his grandson to swim by precept (that beautiful proxy for practice)—at such a time, I say, there lived a remarkably fine trout in that hole. Anglers are notoriously truthful, especially as to what they catch, or even more frequently have not caught. Though I may have written fiction, among many other sins,—as a nice old lady told me once,—now I have to deal with facts; and foul scorn would I count it ever to make believe that I caught that fish. My length at that time was not more than the butt of a four-jointed rod, and all I could catch was a minnow with a pin, which our cook Lydia would not cook, but used to say, "Oh, what a shame, Master Richard! they would have been trout in the summer, please God! if you would only a' let 'em grow on." She is living now, and will bear me out in this.

But upon every great occasion there arises a great man; or to put it more accurately, in the present instance, a mighty and distinguished boy. My father, being the parson of the parish, and getting, need it be said, small pay, took sundry pupils, very pleasant fellows, about to adorn the universities. Among them was the original "Bude Light," as he was satirically called at Cambridge, for he came from Bude, and there was no light in him. Among them also was John Pike, a born Zebedee, if ever there was one.

John Pike was a thick-set younker, with a large and bushy head, keen blue eyes that could see through water, and the proper slouch of shoulder into which great anglers ripen; but greater still are born with it; and of these was Master John. It mattered little what the weather was, and scarcely more as to the time of year, John Pike must have his fishing every day, and on Sundays he read about it, and made flies. All the rest of the time he was thinking about it.

My father was coaching him in the fourth book of the Æneid and all those wonderful speeches of Dido, where passion disdains construction; but the only line Pike cared for was of horsehair. "I fear, Mr. Pike, that you are not giving me your entire attention," my father used to say in his mild dry way; and once when Pike was more than usually abroad, his tutor begged to share his meditations. "Well, sir," said Pike, who was very truthful, "I can see a green drake by the strawberry tree, the first of the season, and your derivation of 'barbarous' put me in mind of my barberry dye." In those days it was a very nice point to get the right tint for the mallard's feather.

No sooner was lesson done than Pike, whose rod was ready upon the lawn, dashed away always for the river, rushing headlong down the hill, and away to the left through a private yard, where "no thoroughfare" was put up, and a big dog stationed to enforce it. But Cerberus himself could not have stopped John Pike; his conscience backed him up in trespass the most sinful when his heart was inditing of a trout upon the rise.

All this, however, is preliminary, as the boy said when he put his father's coat upon his grandfather's tenterhooks, with felonious intent upon his grandmother's apples; the main point to be understood is this, that nothing—neither brazen tower, hundred-eyed Argus, nor Cretan Minotaur—could stop John Pike from getting at a good stickle. But, even as the world knows nothing of its greatest men, its greatest men know nothing of the world beneath their very nose, till fortune sneezes dexter. For two years John Pike must have been whipping the water as hard as Xerxes, without having ever once dreamed of the glorious trout that lived in Crocker's Hole. But why, when he ought to have been at least on bowing terms with every fish as long as his middle finger, why had he failed to know this champion? The answer is simple—because of his short cuts. Flying as he did like an arrow from a bow, Pike used to hit his beloved river at an elbow, some furlong below Crocker's Hole, where a sweet little stickle sailed away down stream, whereas for the length of a meadow upward the water lay smooth, clear, and shallow; therefore the youth, with so little time to spare, rushed into the downward joy.

And here it may be noted that the leading maxim of the present period, that man can discharge his duty only by going counter to the stream, was scarcely mooted in those days. My grandfather (who was a wonderful man, if he was accustomed to fill a cart in two days of fly-fishing on the Barle) regularly fished down stream; and what more than a cartload need anyone put into his basket?

And surely it is more genial and pleasant to behold our friend the river growing and thriving as we go on, strengthening its voice and enlargening its bosom, and sparkling through each successive meadow with richer plenitude of silver, than to trace it against its own grain and good-will toward weakness, and littleness, and immature conceptions.

However, you will say that if John Pike had fished up stream, he would have found this trout much sooner. And that is true; but still, as it was, the trout had more time to grow into such a prize. And the way in which John found him out was this. For some days he had been tormented with a very painful tooth, which even poisoned all the joys of fishing. Therefore he resolved to have it out, and sturdily entered the shop of John Sweetland, the village blacksmith, and there paid his sixpence. Sweetland extracted the teeth of the village, whenever they required it, in the simplest and most effectual way. A piece of fine wire was fastened round the tooth, and the other end round the anvil's nose, then the sturdy blacksmith shut the lower half of his shop door, which was about breast-high, with the patient outside and the anvil within; a strong push of the foot upset the anvil, and the tooth flew out like a well-thrown fly.

When John Pike had suffered this very bravely, "Ah, Master Pike," said the blacksmith, with a grin, "I reckon you won't pull out thic there big vish,"—the smithy commanded a view of the river,—"clever as you be, quite so peart as thiccy."

"What big fish?" asked the boy, with deepest interest, though his mouth was bleeding fearfully.

"Why that girt mortial of a vish as hath his hover in Crocker's Hole. Zum on 'em saith as a' must be a zammon."

Off went Pike with his handkerchief to his mouth, and after him ran Alec Bolt, one of his fellow-pupils, who had come to the shop to enjoy the extraction.

"Oh, my!" was all that Pike could utter, when by craftily posting himself he had obtained a good view of this grand fish.

"I'll lay you a crown you don't catch him!" cried Bolt, an impatient youth, who scorned angling.

"How long will you give me?" asked the wary Pike, who never made rash wagers.

"Oh! till the holidays if you like; or, if that won't do, till Michaelmas."

Now the midsummer holidays were six weeks off—boys used not to talk of "vacations" then, still less of "recesses."

"I think I'll bet you," said Pike, in his slow way, bending forward carefully, with his keen eyes on this monster; "but it would not be fair to take till Michaelmas. I'll bet you a crown that I catch him before the holidays—at least, unless some other fellow does."

PART II.

The day of that most momentous interview must have been the 14th of May. Of the year I will not be so sure; for children take more note of days than of years, for which the latter have their full revenge thereafter. It must have been the 14th, because the morrow was our holiday, given upon the 15th of May, in honour of a birthday.

Now, John Pike was beyond his years wary as well as enterprising, calm as well as ardent, quite as rich in patience as in promptitude and vigour. But Alec Bolt was a headlong youth, volatile, hot, and hasty, fit only to fish the Maëlstrom, or a torrent of new lava. And the moment he had laid that wager he expected his crown piece; though time, as the lawyers phrase it, was "expressly of the essence of the contract." And now he demanded that Pike should spend the holiday in trying to catch that trout.

"I shall not go near him," that lad replied, "until I have got a new collar." No piece of personal adornment was it, without which he would not act, but rather that which now is called the fly-cast, or the gut-cast, or the trace, or what it may be. "And another thing," continued Pike; "the bet is off if you go near him, either now or at any other time, without asking my leave first, and then only going as I tell you."

"What do I want with the great slimy beggar?" the arrogant Bolt made answer. "A good rat is worth fifty of him. No fear of my going near him, Pike. You shan't get out of it that way."

Pike showed his remarkable qualities that day, by fishing exactly as he would have fished without having heard of the great Crockerite. He was up and away upon the mill-stream before breakfast; and the forenoon he devoted to his favourite course—first down the Craddock stream, a very pretty confluent of the Culm, and from its junction, down the pleasant hams, where the river winds toward Uffculme. It was my privilege to accompany this hero, as his humble Sancho; while Bolt and the faster race went up the river ratting. We were back in time to have Pike's trout (which ranged between two ounces and one-half pound) fried for the early dinner; and here it may be lawful to remark that the trout of the Culm are of the very purest excellence, by reason of the flinty bottom, at any rate in these the upper regions. For the valley is the western outlet of the Black-down range, with the Beacon hill upon the north, and Hackpen long ridge to the south; and beyond that again the Whetstone hill, upon whose western end dark port-holes scarped with white grit mark the pits. But flint is the staple of the broad Culm Valley, under good, well-pastured loam; and here are chalcedonies and agate stones.

At dinner everybody had a brace of trout—large for the larger folk, little for the little ones, with coughing and some patting on the back for bones. What of equal purport could the fierce rat-hunter show? Pike explained many points in the history of each fish, seeming to know them none the worse, and love them all the better, for being fried. We banqueted, neither a whit did soul get stinted of banquet impartial. Then the wielder of the magic rod very modestly sought leave of absence at the tea time.

"Fishing again, Mr. Pike, I suppose," my father answered pleasantly; "I used to be fond of it at your age; but never so entirely wrapped up in it as you are."

"No, sir; I am not going fishing again. I want to walk to Wellington, to get some things at Cherry's."

"Books, Mr. Pike? Ah! I am very glad of that. But I fear it can only be fly-books."

"I want a little Horace for eighteen-pence—the Cambridge one just published, to carry in my pocket—and a new hank of gut."

"Which of the two is more important? Put that into Latin, and answer it."

"Utrum pluris facio? Flaccum flocci. Viscera magni."
With this vast effort Pike turned as red as any trout spot.

"After that who could refuse you?" said my father. "You always tell the truth, my boy, in Latin or in English."

Although it was a long walk, some fourteen miles to Wellington and back, I got permission to go with Pike; and as we crossed the bridge and saw the tree that overhung Crocker's Hole, I begged him to show me that mighty fish.

"Not a bit of it," he replied. "It would bring the blackguards. If the blackguards once find him out, it is all over with him."

"The blackguards are all in factory now, and I am sure they cannot see us from the windows. They won't be out till five o'clock."

With the true liberality of young England, which abides even now as large and glorious as ever, we always called the free and enlightened operatives of the period by the courteous name above set down, and it must be acknowledged that some of them deserved it, although perhaps they poached with less of science than their sons. But the cowardly murder of fish by liming the water was already prevalent.

Yielding to my request and perhaps his own desire—manfully kept in check that morning—Pike very carefully approached that pool, commanding me to sit down while he reconnoitred from the meadow upon the right bank of the stream. And the place which had so sadly quenched the fire of the poor baker's love filled my childish heart with dread and deep wonder at the cruelty of women. But as for John Pike, all he thought of was the fish and the best way to get at him.

Very likely that hole is "holed out" now, as the Yankees well express it, or at any rate changed out of knowledge. Even in my time a very heavy flood entirely altered its character; but to the eager eye of Pike it seemed pretty much as follows, and possibly it may have come to such a form again:

The river, after passing though a hurdle fence at the head of the meadow, takes a little turn or two of bright and shallow indifference, then gathers itself into a good strong slide, as if going down a slope instead of steps. The right bank is high and beetles over with yellow loam and grassy fringe; but the other side is of flinty shingle, low and bare and washed by floods. At the end of this rapid, the stream turns sharply under an ancient alder tree into a large, deep, calm repose, cool, unruffled, and sheltered from the sun by branch and leaf—and that is the hole of poor Crocker.

At the head of the pool (where the hasty current rushes in so eagerly, with noisy excitement and much ado) the quieter waters from below, having rested and enlarged themselves, come lapping up round either curve, with some recollection of their past career, the hoary experience of foam. And sidling toward the new arrival of the impulsive column, where they meet it, things go on, which no man can describe without his mouth being full of water. A "V" is formed, a fancy letter V, beyond any designer's tracery, and even beyond his imagination, a perpetually fluctuating limpid wedge, perpetually crenelled and rippled into by little ups and downs that try to make an impress, but can only glide away upon either side or sink in dimples under it. And here a gray bough of the ancient alder stretches across, like a thirsty giant's arm, and makes it a very ticklish place to throw a fly. Yet this was the very spot our John Pike must put his fly into, or lose his crown.

Because the great tenant of Crocker's Hole, who allowed no other fish to wag a fin there, and from strict monopoly had grown so fat, kept his victualing yard—if so low an expression can be used concerning him—within about a square yard of this spot. He had a sweet hover, both for rest and recreation, under the bank, in a placid antre, where the water made no noise, but tickled his belly in digestive ease. The loftier the character is of any being, the slower and more dignified his movements are. No true psychologist could have believed—as Sweetland the blacksmith did, and Mr. Pook the tinman—that this trout could ever be the embodiment of Crocker. For this was the last trout in the universal world to drown himself for love; if truly any trout has done so.

"You may come now, and try to look along my back," John Pike, with a reverential whisper, said to me. "Now don't be in a hurry, young stupid; kneel down. He is not to be disturbed at his dinner, mind. You keep behind me, and look along my back; I never clapped eyes on such a whopper."

I had to kneel down in a tender reminiscence of pasture land, and gaze carefully; and not having eyes like those of our Zebedee (who offered his spine for a camera, as he crawled on all fours in front of me), it took me a long time to descry an object most distinct to all who have that special gift of piercing with their eyes the water. See what is said upon this subject in that delicious book, "The Gamekeeper at Home."

"You are no better than a muff," said Pike, and it was not in my power to deny it.

"If the sun would only leave off," I said. But the sun, who was having a very pleasant play with the sparkle of the water and the twinkle of the leaves, had no inclination to leave off yet, but kept the rippling crystal in a dance of flashing facets, and the quivering verdure in a steady flush of gold.

But suddenly a May-fly, a luscious gray-drake, richer and more delicate than canvas-back or woodcock, with a dart and a leap and a merry zigzag, began to enjoy a little game above the stream. Rising and falling like a gnat, thrilling her gauzy wings, and arching her elegant pellucid frame, every now and then she almost dipped her three long tapering whisks into the dimples of the water.

"He sees her! He'll have her as sure as a gun!" cried Pike, with a gulp, as if he himself were "rising." "Now, can you see him, stupid?"

"Crikey, crokums!" I exclaimed, with classic elegance; "I have seen that long thing for five minutes; but I took it for a tree."

"You little"—animal quite early in the alphabet—"now don't you stir a peg, or I'll dig my elbow into you."

The great trout was stationary almost as a stone, in the middle of the "V" above described. He was gently fanning with his large clear fins, but holding his own against the current mainly by the wagging of his broad-fluked tail. As soon as my slow eyes had once defined him, he grew upon them mightily, moulding himself in the matrix of the water, as a thing put into jelly does. And I doubt whether even John Pike saw him more accurately than I did. His size was such, or seemed to be such, that I fear to say a word about it; not because language does not contain the word, but from dread of exaggeration. But his shape and colour may be reasonably told without wounding the feeling of an age whose incredulity springs from self-knowledge.

His head was truly small, his shoulders vast; the spring of his back was like a rainbow when the sun is southing; the generous sweep of his deep elastic belly, nobly pulped out with rich nurture, showed what the power of his brain must be, and seemed to undulate, time for time, with the vibrant vigilance of his large wise eyes. His latter end was consistent also. An elegant taper run of counter, coming almost to a cylinder, as a mackered does, boldly developed with a hugeous spread to a glorious amplitude of swallow-tail. His colour was all that can well be desired, but ill-described by any poor word-palette. Enough that he seemed to tone away from olive and umber, with carmine stars, to glowing gold and soft pure silver, mantled with a subtle flush of rose and fawn and opal.

Swoop came a swallow, as we gazed, and was gone with a flick, having missed the May-fly. But the wind of his passage, or the skir of wing, struck the merry dancer down, so that he fluttered for one instant on the wave, and that instant was enough. Swift as the swallow, and more true of aim, the great trout made one dart, and a sound, deeper than a tinkle, but as silvery as a bell, rang the poor ephemerid's knell. The rapid water scarcely showed a break; but a bubble sailed down the pool, and the dark hollow echoed with the music of a rise.

"He knows how to take a fly," said Pike; "he has had too many to be tricked with mine. Have him I must; but how ever shall I do it?"

All the way to Wellington he uttered not a word, but shambled along with a mind full of care. When I ventured to look up now and then, to surmise what was going on beneath his hat, deeply-set eyes and a wrinkled forehead, relieved at long intervals by a solid shake, proved that there are meditations deeper than those of philosopher or statesman.

PART III.

Surely no trout could have been misled by the artificial May-fly of that time, unless he were either a very young fish, quite new to entomology, or else one afflicted with a combination of myopy and bulimy. Even now there is room for plenty of improvement in our counterfeit presentment; but in those days the body was made with yellow mohair, ribbed with red silk and gold twist, and as thick as a fertile bumble-bee. John Pike perceived that to offer such a thing to Crocker's trout would probably consign him—even if his great stamina should over-get the horror—to an uneatable death, through just and natural indignation. On the other hand, while the May-fly lasted, a trout so cultured, so highly refined, so full of light and sweetness, would never demean himself to low bait, or any coarse son of a maggot.

Meanwhile Alec Bolt allowed poor Pike no peaceful thought, no calm absorption of high mind into the world of flies, no placid period of cobblers' wax, floss-silk, turned hackles, and dubbing. For in making of flies John Pike had his special moments of inspiration, times of clearer insight into the everlasting verities, times of brighter conception and more subtle execution, tails of more elastic grace and heads of a neater and nattier expression. As a poet labours at one immortal line, compressing worlds of wisdom into the music of ten syllables, so toiled the patient Pike about the fabric of a fly comprising all the excellence that ever sprang from maggot. Yet Bolt rejoiced to jerk his elbow at the moment of sublimest art. And a swarm of flies was blighted thus.

Peaceful, therefore, and long-suffering, and full of resignation as he was, John Pike came slowly to the sad perception that arts avail not without arms. The elbow, so often jerked, at last took a voluntary jerk from the shoulder and Alec Bolt lay prostrate, with his right eye full of cobbler's wax. This put a desirable check upon his energies for a week or more, and by that time Pike had flown his fly.

When the honeymoon of spring and summer (which they are now too fashionable to celebrate in this country), the heyday of the whole year marked by the budding of the wild rose, the start of the wheatear from its sheath, the feathering of the lesser plantain, and flowering of the meadow-sweet, and, foremost for the angler's joy, the caracole of May-flies—when these things are to be seen and felt (which has not happened at all this year), then rivers should be mild and bright, skies blue and white with fleecy cloud, the west wind blowing softly, and the trout in charming appetite.

On such a day came Pike to the bank of Culm, with a loudly beating heart. A fly there is, not ignominious, or of cowdab origin, neither gross and heavy-bodied, from cradlehood of slimy stones, nor yet of menacing aspect and suggesting deeds of poison, but elegant, bland, and of sunny nature, and obviously good to eat. Him or her—why quest we which?—the shepherd of the dale, contemptuous of gender, except in his own species, has called, and as long as they two coexist will call, the "Yellow Sally." A fly that does not waste the day in giddy dances and the fervid waltz, but undergoes family incidents with decorum and discretion. He or she, as the case may be,—for the natural history of the river bank is a book to come hereafter, and of fifty men who make flies not one knows the name of the fly he is making,—in the early morning of June, or else in the second quarter of the afternoon, this Yellow Sally fares abroad, with a nice well-ordered flutter.

Despairing of the May-fly, as it still may be despaired of, Pike came down to the river with his master-piece of portraiture. The artificial Yellow Sally is generally always—as they say in Cheshire—a mile or more too yellow. On the other hand, the "Yellow Dun" conveys no idea of any Sally. But Pike had made a very decent Sally, not perfect (for he was young as well as wise), but far above any counterfeit to be had in fishing-tackle shops.

How he made it, he told nobody. But if he lives now, as I hope he does, any of my readers may ask him through the G. P. O., and hope to get an answer.

It fluttered beautifully on the breeze, and in such living form, that a brother or sister Sally came up to see it, and went away sadder and wiser. Then Pike said: "Get away, you young wretch," to your humble servant who tells this tale; yet being better than his words, allowed that pious follower to lie down upon his digestive organs and with deep attention watch. There must have been great things to see, but to see them so was difficult. And if I huddle up what happened, excitement also shares the blame.

Pike had fashioned well the time and manner of this overture. He knew that the giant Crockerite was satiate now with May-flies, or began to find their flavour failing, as happens to us with asparagus, marrow-fat peas, or strawberries, when we have had a month of them. And he thought that the first Yellow Sally of the season, inferior though it were, might have the special charm of novelty. With the skill of a Zulu, he stole up through the branches over the lower pool till he came to a spot where a yard-wide opening gave just space for spring of rod. Then he saw his desirable friend at dinner, wagging his tail, as a hungry gentleman dining with the Lord Mayor agitates his coat. With one dexterous whirl, untaught by any of the many books upon the subject, John Pike laid his Yellow Sally (for he cast with one fly only) as lightly as gossamer upon the rapid, about a yard in front of the big trout's head. A moment's pause, and then, too quick for words, was the things that happened.

A heavy plunge was followed by a fearful rush. Forgetful of current the river was ridged, as if with a plough driven under it; the strong line, though given out as fast as might be, twanged like a harp-string as it cut the wave, and then Pike stood up, like a ship dismasted, with the butt of his rod snapped below the ferrule. He had one of those foolish things, just invented, a hollow butt of hickory; and the finial ring of his spare top looked out, to ask what had happened to the rest of it. "Bad luck!" cried the fisherman; "but never mind, I shall have him next time, to a certainty."

When this great issue came to be considered, the cause of it was sadly obvious. The fish, being hooked, had made off with the rush of a shark for the bottom of the pool. A thicket of saplings below the alder tree had stopped the judicious hooker from all possibility of following; and when he strove to turn him by elastic pliance, his rod broke at the breach of pliability. "I have learned a sad lesson," said John Pike, looking sadly.

How many fellows would have given up this matter, and glorified themselves for having hooked so grand a fish, while explaining that they must have caught him, if they could have done it! But Pike only told me not to say a word about it, and began to make ready for another tug of war. He made himself a splice-rod, short and handy, of well-seasoned ash, with a stout top of bamboo, tapered so discreetly, and so balanced in its spring, that verily it formed an arc, with any pressure on it, as perfect as a leafy poplar in a stormy summer. "Now break it if you can," he said, "by any amount of rushes; I'll hook you by your jacket collar; you cut away now, and I'll land you."

This was highly skilful, and he did it many times; and whenever I was landed well, I got a lollypop, so that I was careful not to break his tackle. Moreover he made him a landing net, with a kidney-bean stick, a ring of wire, and his own best nightcap of strong cotton net. Then he got the farmer's leave, and lopped obnoxious bushes; and now the chiefest question was: what bait, and when to offer it? In spite of his sad rebuff, the spirit of John Pike had been equable. The genuine angling mind is steadfast, large, and self-supported, and to the vapid, ignominious chaff, tossed by swine upon the idle wind, it pays as much heed as a big trout does to a dance of midges. People put their fingers to their noses and said: "Master Pike, have you caught him yet?" and Pike only answered: "Wait a bit." If ever this fortitude and perseverance is to be recovered as the English Brand (the one thing that has made us what we are, and may yet redeem us from niddering shame), a degenerate age should encourage the habit of fishing and never despairing. And the brightest sign yet for our future is the increasing demand for hooks and gut.

Pike fished in a manlier age, when nobody would dream of cowering from a savage because he was clever at skulking; and when, if a big fish broke the rod, a stronger rod was made for him, according to the usage of Great Britain. And though the young angler had been defeated, he did not sit down and have a good cry over it.

About the second week in June, when the May-fly had danced its day, and died,—for the season was an early one,—and Crocker's trout had recovered from the wound to his feelings and philanthropy, there came a night of gentle rain, of pleasant tinkling upon window ledges, and a soothing patter among young leaves, and the Culm was yellow in the morning. "I mean to do it this afternoon," Pike whispered to me, as he came back panting. "When the water clears there will be a splendid time."

The lover of the rose knows well a gay voluptuous beetle, whose pleasure is to lie embedded in a fount of beauty. Deep among the incurving petals of the blushing fragrance, he loses himself in his joys sometimes, till a breezy waft reveals him. And when the sunlight breaks upon his luscious dissipation, few would have the heart to oust him, such a gem from such a setting. All his back is emerald sparkles; all his front red Indian gold, and here and there he grows white spots to save the eye from aching. Pike put his finger in and fetched him out, and offered him a little change of joys, by putting a Limerick hook through his thorax, and bringing it out between his elytra. *Cetonia aurata* liked it not, but pawed the air very naturally, and fluttered with his wings attractively.

"I meant to have tried with a fern-web", said the angler; "until I saw one of these beggars this morning. If he works like that upon the water, he will do. It was hopeless to try artificials again. What a lovely colour the water is! Only three days now to the holidays. I have run it very close. You be ready, younker."

With these words he stepped upon a branch of the alder, for the tone of the waters allowed approach, being soft and sublustrous, without any mud. Also Master Pike's own tone was such as becomes the fisherman, calm, deliberate, free from nerve, but full of eye and muscle. He stepped upon the alder bough to get as near as might be to the fish, for he could not cast this beetle like a fly; it must be dropped gently and allowed to play. "You may come and look," he said to me; "when the water is so, they have no eyes in their tails."

The rose-beetle trod upon the water prettily, under a lively vibration, and he looked quite as happy, and considerably more active, than when he had been cradled in the anthers of the rose. To the eye of a fish he was a strong individual, fighting courageously with the current, but sure to be beaten through lack of fins; and mercy suggested, as well as appetite, that the proper solution was to gulp him.

"Hooked him in the gullet. He can't get off!" cried John Pike, labouring to keep his nerves under; "every inch of tackle is as strong as a bell-pull. Now, if I don't land him, I will never fish again!"

Providence, which had constructed Pike, foremost of all things, for lofty angling—disdainful of worm and even minnow —Providence, I say, at this adjuration, pronounced that Pike must catch that trout. Not many anglers are heaven-born; and for one to drop off the hook halfway through his teens would be infinitely worse than to slay the champion trout. Pike felt the force of this, and rushing through the rushes, shouted: "I am sure to have him, Dick! Be ready with my nightcap."

Rod in a bow, like a springle-riser; line on the hum, like

the string of Paganini; winch on the gallop, like a harpoon wheel, Pike, the head-centre of everything, dashing through thick and thin, and once taken overhead—for he jumped into the hole, when he must have lost him else, but the fish too impetuously towed him out, and made off in passion for another pool, when, if he had only retired to his hover, the angler might have shared the baker's fate—all these things (I tell you, for they all come up again, as if the day were yesterday) so scared me of my never very steadfast wits, that I could only holloa! But one thing I did, I kept the nightcap ready.

"He is pretty nearly spent, I do believe," said Pike; and his voice was like balm of Gilead, as we came to Farmer Anning's meadow, a quarter of a mile below Crocker's Hole. "Take it coolly, my dear boy, and we shall be safe to have him."

Never have I felt, through forty years, such tremendous responsibility. I had not the faintest notion how to use a landing net; but a mighty general directed me. "Don't let him see it; don't let him see it! Don't clap it over him; go under him, you stupid! If he makes another rush, he will get off, after all. Bring it up his tail. Well done! You have him!"

The mighty trout lay in the nightcap of Pike, which was half a fathom long, with a tassel at the end, for his mother had made it in the winter evenings. "Come and hold the rod, if you can't lift him," my master shouted, and so I did. Then, with both arms straining, and his mouth wide open, John Pike made a mighty sweep, and we both fell upon the grass and rolled, with the giant of the deep flapping heavily between us, and no power left to us, except to cry, "Hurrah!"

THE END.

131

Lightning Source UK Ltd.
Milton Keynes UK
UKHW022143171019
351815UK00005B/194/P

9 781388 239589